The First Time Ever Published!

The Third Book in the Brand New Classic Diner Mystery
Series from Jessica Beck, the
New York Times Bestselling Author of The Donut Shop
Mysteries!

The Classic Diner Mystery Series

Book 3

A KILLER CAKE

by
Jessica Beck

Books by Jessica Beck

The Classic Diner Mysteries
A Chili Death
A Deadly Beef
A Killer Cake
A Baked Ham (coming 2013)

The Donut Shop Mysteries
Glazed Murder
Fatally Frosted
Sinister Sprinkles
Evil Éclairs
Tragic Toppings
Killer Crullers
Drop Dead Chocolate
Powdered Peril
Illegally Iced

To all the waitresses who have ever called me Honey,
Sweetie, or Dear!

A KILLER CAKE: Copyright © 2012

All rights reserved.

Cozy Publishing

Recipes included in this book are to be recreated at the reader's own risk. The author is not responsible for any damage, medical or otherwise, created as a result of reproducing these recipes. It is the responsibility of the reader to ensure that none of the ingredients are detrimental to their health, and the author will not be held liable in any way for any problems that might arise from following the included recipes.

Chapter 1

The instant the cannon went off, everybody gathered in the town square for Jasper Fork's bicentennial celebration believed that the Civil War weapon was responsible for killing Roy Thompson. After all, his seat at the long table filled with folks eating lunch and having dessert was in the direct line of fire of the old weaponry.

However, it turned out that the chamber was indeed empty when it had been fired, and though either the noise or the ensuing shock wave of the explosion could have been enough to stop his heart, neither had been the cause of his death.

It wasn't long before I found myself wishing that the cannon had indeed been the reason for Roy's demise. Soon enough, word spread through town like a hurricane that what really did him in was the Jasper Fork bicentennial cake. The fact that my diner had provided it for the festivities meant that once again, my family was in the crosshairs of another murder investigation.

My name is Victoria Nelson, and along with my sometimes dysfunctional but always loving family, I run The Charming Moose Diner. The place was named after my grandfather a long time ago, and I loved the distinctive moniker. It's easy enough to explain how we ended up volunteering to bake the murder weapon for our town's celebration, but it might be better to go back to the day before Roy collapsed after taking his first bite of our cake.

"Moose, we're going to do this free of charge, and that's final," I told my grandfather during the lull between lunch and dinner as we brainstormed about what kind of cake Greg should make as our donation to the celebration. "Even if it *weren't* good for our image, which we both know it is, I feel as though we owe it to the community."

"Victoria, I'm as civic-minded as the next man, but would it hurt for the Celebration Fund to at least cover our expenses? We're talking about a great deal of materials to make as much cake as they're asking us to provide, and I'm willing to bet that not *everyone* in town is doing something for nothing."

I looked over at my husband, who was at his regular station working the grill in the kitchen of The Charming Moose. "Greg, I'm getting hoarse. Why don't you try talking to him?"

My husband grinned at me happily as he said, "Oh, no. Not me. I'm not about to get between the two of you. You can handle the executive decisions around here on your own. I'm just a fry cook."

"You're a great deal more than that, and you know it," I said. I owned the place on paper these days, but I couldn't run it without Greg and my mother, who also worked the grill, not to mention the two women we had on staff who came in to waitress. Even Moose and my grandmother, Martha, helped out on occasion, and if the circumstances were dire enough, my father would pitch in, though he'd had his turn running the diner before I'd taken over, and everyone agreed that hadn't been a good match at all.

"Sure, I know that I'm handy back here," Greg said as he flipped a burger, "but I have no desire to get involved in your discussion. I'm happy to bake whatever you ask me to, but that's the extent of how much I'm willing to get involved."

"Victoria, let's be reasonable," my grandfather said in that calming voice he sometimes used to try to get his way. "What would it hurt to ask the committee for a few dollars so that we at least meet our expenses?"

I shook my head. "You don't get it, Moose. You know as well as I do that we've had some trouble lately with our reputation in Jasper Fork. I don't know *exactly* why we were cursed, but murder has been finding its way to our doorstep much too much over the past several months, and I'm beginning to wonder what folks are starting to say about us. Wouldn't it be nice if, for once, they were openly complimenting our contribution to the celebration, instead of whispering behind our backs that there's a dark shadow over our threshold these days?"

"Who's saying that?" Moose asked a little heatedly, and there was no doubt in my mind that he was ready to go out and confront whoever I named. What my grandfather lacked in subtlety, he made up for with a blunt force that was nearly unstoppable. I liked to think that I was a little more gifted in the finesse department, but that was what made us such a good team. We'd solved the murders that had come our way in the past, or at least survived them, which was saying something, but what I really loved doing was running The Charming Moose. Sure, my hours were crazy, and the demands could be overwhelming at times, but there was nowhere else I'd rather be than at the register or behind the counter serving our customers.

"I'm sorry to disappoint you, but I don't have a list of names for you," I said with a smile as I patted his shoulder. "I'm just saying that it wouldn't be that hard to believe that it's happening, would it, given our recent history?"

"I don't know," Moose said after a moment's pause. "Maybe you're right."

It took me a full second to realize that he'd just agreed with me. "Pardon me? Would you mind saying that one more time?"

"Don't ask me to repeat it," my grandfather said with a grin. "I'm not sure that I can bring myself to do it."

I kissed his cheek. "Thanks for saying it even once. I won't ask you to say it again. Moose, don't worry so much. We can afford to do this on the house, and the goodwill we're going to get out of it will be totally worth it. Now, what kind of cake should we make?"

"I don't know; what's the cheapest one we can do, Greg?" he asked my husband.

Greg just laughed at the question and continued to work on the meal orders that were in line. Sometimes it drove me crazy when he acted that way, but there were definitely times when I admired my husband's ability to gleefully ignore any and all questions he didn't want to answer.

There were moments when I wished that I knew how to do it myself.

"Forget about what it costs," I told Greg. "Just make something that we'll be proud to contribute."

"You're both in luck. I might be able to satisfy your requests with one cake," he said as he plated some meatloaf, mashed potatoes, and green beans. It was our daily special today, and Greg was always ready to serve an army when it came up in the rotation. It was that popular. "I could always make my famous Lemon Drop cake with cream cheese icing. Would that be okay?"

"It's perfect," Moose and I said in unison, and then we all shared a smile. It appeared that The Charming Moose's contribution was going to put our best foot forward to the community again. I just hoped it made folks forget how often murder had played a part in our lives recently.

"What a jerk," Jenny Hollister said as she stormed into the kitchen a little after six. "I'll tell you one thing. He's lucky I didn't slam that pie into his face."

Jenny was our late-afternoon to early-evening waitress at the diner, a sweet and good-natured college student who normally didn't have a cross word for anyone.

"Who are you talking about?" I asked as stood. I'd been keeping Greg company for a few minutes in the kitchen, something I tried to do at least once every evening. From where I sat, I could see the cash register through the pickup window, and the front door as well, so if Jenny ever needed me, I'd be right there.

"Roy Thompson," she said, saying his name as though it were something bad that might be contagious.

"What did he do this time?" I asked. Roy was an older

man, somewhere in his early seventies, who owned quite a bit of land around town. Rumor was that he'd never been all that pleasant to be around, and clearly, age had done nothing to mellow him. It had been my experience that some older men grew older with grace and became a joy to have at our diner with their pleasant demeanors, but others didn't take to the aging process nearly as well. Roy was definitely in that camp. Not a week went by that he didn't complain about something he ordered at the diner, and apparently, today was no exception.

"He said that the only thing worse here than the food was my service. I saw the money he put beside his ticket, and it's pretty clear that he's leaving me a grand total of seven cents as a tip."

"We'll just see about that," Greg said as his smile disappeared and he reached for a nearby meat cleaver. "I'm fed up with that man, and I'm going to settle things once and for all."

"Hang on just a second," I said as I stood between my husband and the door to the dining room. "I know how protective you are of Jenny and Ellen, but I'll handle this. After all, it's my responsibility, remember? You deal with the kitchen, and everything else is mine."

Greg frowned as the cleaver bobbed up and down in his hand. "Victoria, why don't you let me take a swing at it myself just this once?"

"With that?" I asked with a smile as I took the cleaver out of his hand and put it on the counter. "Greg, I don't need weapons to shred the man. I happen to agree with you, though. Enough is enough."

Jenny spoke up in Roy's defense, to my amazement. "Listen, maybe I overreacted. He's not that bad. It just hit me wrong tonight. There's no need for either one of you to say anything to him. I'm fine, really."

I shook my head. "You're not the only one he's antagonized here," I said. "I appreciate the sentiment, but we don't need that man's business any more if he can't learn to behave himself." I walked out of the kitchen and headed straight for Roy's table. It was remarkable how well the man had aged; he was still as handsome as ever. It was just a shame that what was on the inside didn't match the exterior. The diner had half a dozen other diners there enjoying a meal, and the second they saw the expression on my face, all the other conversations shut down instantly. It was pretty clear that we were going to have an audience, but frankly, at that point I didn't care.

"I understand that you have a problem with the food *and* the service at The Charming Moose this evening," I said firmly.

He grinned at me with a wicked smile. Evidently this was better than he'd been hoping for. "As a matter of fact, I'm not sure which is worse. The food is swill, and the service is virtually nonexistent. What's the matter? Did Jenny come crying to you about me airing a few legitimate complaints?"

I did my best to keep my temper in check as I said, "Roy, we've had this conversation before, and frankly, I'm tired of having it. If you don't like the food or the service here, why do you insist on coming back week after week?"

"Honestly, I keep hoping that either the food or the service will improve, but neither one has managed to do it yet."

"That's it," I said as I picked up his check, ignoring his careful stack of ones and the change sitting right beside it, and tore the bill in two. "Don't worry about your check. This meal's on the house."

Before I could finish, Roy smiled brightly at me. "It's about time you admitted your mistakes and actually felt guilty about what you do here."

I smiled right back at him, but there was not an ounce of warmth in it. "You don't get it, Roy. The reason this meal is free is because it's the last time you're ever going to eat here. As of right now, you are no longer welcome at The Charming Moose, at least not until your manners improve. Do you understand what I'm telling you?"

"You can't keep me out just because I'm honest!" he said, stammering in anger. Not many folks were willing to stand up to the rich man, but I was. If he didn't like it, what could he do, refuse to come back? I'd already taken care of that. As much as I hated banning a paying customer, this man needed it if anyone ever had.

"That's where you're wrong. Read the sign under the register," I said as I pointed toward it. Moose had put up the declaration before he'd first opened the diner's front door, and it gave us the right to refuse service to anyone, for any reason. It was a rare day that we enforced it, but I was always glad that it was there, just in case.

"I'm afraid that you are the one who is mistaken. We'll see about the legality of your sign. You can trust that my lawyers will be here first thing tomorrow morning," Roy said as he stood.

"You can send a judge on your behalf if you'd like, but my decision stands. I'll serve them all as long as they're polite, but I won't change my mind." I shouldn't have added the next bit, and I knew it as soon as the words left my lips, but I couldn't help myself. "Now, are you going to go peacefully, or do I have to get my husband and his meat cleaver out here to persuade you to leave a place where you're not welcome?"

Roy clearly didn't like that, but he got up and headed for the door anyway.

I couldn't let it go at that, though. I had to add, "Hey, Roy. You forgot your money."

"Keep it," he growled, and then he left.

I watched him go, and then I was startled to hear a burst of applause coming from the dining room as well as the kitchen, where the door stood open as Greg and Jenny joined in. I was a little embarrassed by the display as I made my way back into the kitchen.

"I suppose you two saw all of that," I said to my staff.

"I just wish I had it on tape," Greg said.

Jenny stepped forward and hugged me. "Nobody's ever defended me like that before. You rock, Victoria."

I didn't want her to know that I'd actually done it for the diner, but then again, she was just as much a part of The Charming Moose as anyone else on staff, including me and my family, so in a way, it was true enough.

Moose came by as we were closing. He had an odd expression on his face. "Can we have a word, Victoria?" he asked me.

"Sure, fire away," I said as I locked the door behind him and flipped the sign from Open to Closed. "What's up?"

"I understand you had some words with Roy Thompson earlier."

"As a matter of fact, I threw him out," I said adamantly. "Do you have a problem with that, Moose?"

He couldn't hold back his smile any longer. "Are you kidding?" my grandfather said with a hearty laugh. "I'm proud of you. Victoria, I'd give you a medal if I had one. Thompson's been asking for that for years, and I for one am glad that you finally pulled the trigger."

I wasn't as confident in my decision as I had been, so it was good to hear that Moose approved. During the hour since I'd booted Roy Thompson from the diner, I'd had time to mull things over, and I was more than a little worried about the barrage of attorneys I was certain Roy had at his disposal. In hindsight, it was almost as though I'd gone out of my way to alienate the man, practically daring him to sue us. "Aren't you worried about the ramifications?" I asked him.

"I heard his threat of bringing a thousand lawyers after us, but we've got Rebecca, so why should we worry?"

"Is that what folks are saying? He never mentioned a specific number."

"You know how folks are around here," Moose said with a laugh. "By tomorrow morning, it will be up to ten thousand, and by tomorrow night, I'm willing to bet that it will top a million."

"Well, we all know that he has money enough to afford whatever he wants to do to us."

Moose put his arm around my shoulder. "Don't worry so much. Tonight, you did more for The Charming Moose's goodwill than us baking a thousand cakes. Speaking of which, has Greg gotten started yet?"

"He's about to put the first batch in the oven," I said.

"How many is he making?"

"We figure half a dozen sheet cakes should do the trick," I said. "He'll be up half the night baking, and I'm going to stay here with him."

"Care to make it a party?" Moose suggested. "We can call your mother, and with two of them working, they can cut that time in half."

"She's already on her way," I said. Mom worked the grill during the morning shift, and she was nearly as good as my husband, but when it came to baking, I had to give Greg the edge.

"I'll call Martha, and if we can get your dad to come down, too, we'll make it a family reunion. There's no reason in the world that we shouldn't have a little party of our own."

"You're truly not upset about the way I treated Roy Thompson?" I asked him.

"Not even the slightest little bit," he said with a grin. "Worst case scenario, if we go down for it, we'll all go down together."

"Somehow I don't find that all that comforting," I said.

"Well, you should. Together, we're all much more than what the diner is; you should know that."

"Thanks," I said. I loved my grandfather dearly. He had a habit of tweaking me in all the right places at times, but I also knew that, short of my husband and my parents, I had no bigger supporter in the world.

"You're most welcome," he said. "Now, let's play something festive on the juke box. I feel like having a party."

As Moose perused our latest titles, I felt my spirits start to buoy. Chances were that Roy would forget all about us by morning, but even if he did bring his lawyers down on us, we'd face them all, together.

Besides, what good was it to have an attorney as a best friend if I didn't utilize her skills every now and then?

Chapter 2

"I can't believe how many people are here, considering how chilly it is," I told Greg the next day as we wandered around the town square together, bundled up and holding hands as we made our way through the crowds. It was a rare treat for us to be able to close the diner at noon for two hours, but it was a long-standing tradition to lock our doors every year during the height of the celebration on March 11th, from the first year my grandfather opened The Charming Moose, and I fully endorsed the arrangement. The residents of Jasper Fork held a massive birthday party for our city every year, and for the bicentennial, we were all really getting into the spirit of things. The road leading into the main square was closed off to cars with bright yellow sawhorses, and a police officer was stationed at each point as well, just in case. Vendors were set up everywhere, offering everything from baked goods to sunglasses to homemade candles, and the food! It was a delightful walk full of guilty pleasures everywhere in sight, offering funnel cakes, caramel apples, and massive turkey legs. Greg was wrestling with one of those as we walked, and I was honestly surprised that he didn't need both hands to handle it.

"Want a bite?" he asked as he offered it to me.

"No, I'd better not."

He grinned at my refusal. "Are you saving room for another ear of corn?" That was my favorite offering, roasted corn on the cob drizzled with melted butter. Where they got fresh corn this time of year, I had no idea, nor did I care. All I knew was that it was delicious.

"Actually, if you ever get finished with that giant leg of yours, I thought we might split a funnel cake."

"Victoria, you never finish one of these, you just decide to abandon it." He took one last bite, and then discarded the remains in a nearby trashcan. They were placed every ten feet throughout the square, and I still wondered if there would be enough. "Besides, I thought you were going to have some of the cake I made for dessert."

"Absolutely," I said, "but I can have that whenever I want. A funnel cake, on the other hand, is something I allow myself just once a year."

"Hey, I'm honored that you're willing to share it with me, then."

"I never promised that it would be an even split, did I?" I asked with a grin.

"No, if I get two bites, I'll be a happy man."

"I believe I can sacrifice that much," I said with a grin, though it instantly disappeared as Roy Thompson approached us displaying a plate of his own.

"Thanks for the cake," Roy said as he waved a piece of Greg's offering right under my nose. "It looks delicious."

"You're not allowed to eat that," I said as I jerked the plate right out of his hands.

"You don't have any right to keep me from it!" Roy said as he snatched the cake right back.

Sheriff Croft must have been standing nearby, though I hadn't realized it until he stepped in between us. "What's going on here, folks?"

"He can't have that cake," I said a little shrilly. I knew the moment I said it how petty it sounded, but I couldn't help myself. I'd banned Roy for good reason, and I didn't like seeing him circumventing my position so easily.

"That cake is there for the public," Roy said, shielding the slice from me as he spoke. "Anybody can have a piece."

"I'm sorry, but he's right, Victoria," the sheriff said.

"I know that," I said in disgust. "I don't have to like it, though, do I? Come on, Greg. Let's go."

The sheriff nodded, and he most likely assumed that the confrontation was over.

It would have been, too, if Roy had kept his mouth shut. He didn't, though. "My, this cake is delicious," Roy said as he took a bite.

"Keep walking," Greg said softly as he tugged at my hand. I hadn't even realized that I had stopped until he did that. "It's just not worth it."

"I hate that he's eating your cake," I whispered.

"I know, but let's not let it spoil our fun."

I resolved to do as Greg suggested, and as we made our way around the booths, I tried my best to forget all about Roy Thompson.

Half an hour later, Mayor Simon Murphy got onto the stage and tapped the microphone. As he did at every public event, he asked the crowd, "Is this thing on?"

Everybody roared, "Yes," and the mayor smiled. The mayor's job was part-time, and paid just a small annual stipend. For his livelihood, the mayor made beautiful, museum-quality furniture that offered rich wood and simple lines. Greg and I had a mahogany nightstand that Simon had made, and it was by far the nicest piece we owned. We wouldn't have been able to afford even that if Simon hadn't drastically reduced its price based on a flaw in it he perceived that we still couldn't find.

"Thanks for coming to the Jasper Fork Bicentennial Celebration," he said, and the crowd applauded and hooted their response. "Everyone, I've got quite a surprise that I'm honored to finally be able to share with you all. We've made it a point to keep this quiet, but it's finally time to announce it. As a special treat, I'd now like to ask the VFW to fire the Civil War cannon in tribute to our fair city, so cover your ears and duck, everybody. I've been told that it's going to be quite a big bang."

I turned to look around, and as I scanned the crowds, I noticed that sitting at a long table directly in the line of fire was Roy Thompson. He was grinning at me as he happily savored every bite of the cake that he didn't deserve to be eating. I decided not to give him the satisfaction of reacting, so I turned to the cannon as several older men in Civil War uniforms prepared to fire it. I was amazed that they were able to get the thing to work, especially since they couldn't have test fired it without giving the surprise away.

I saw Rooster Hicks lower the lit taper to the fuse, and I covered my ears. It seemed to take forever for the light to reach the powder, and I nearly lowered my hands a time or two. When the cannon finally exploded into life, the ground shook, and a great plume of white smoke raced from the barrel.

In the deafening silence that followed, I was just lowering my hands from my ears when I heard someone scream, "Roy Thompson's been shot!"

I looked over at Roy, and sure enough, his body was slumped down in front of him, his face buried squarely in the center of what was left of our cake.

The paramedics on hand nearby rushed to Roy's body even as the sheriff and his deputies leapt into action. A few folks who'd been nearby were trying to get away from the action, but Sheriff Croft was too quick to let anyone escape.

"Did that cannon really just kill him?" I asked Greg.

"I can't imagine they would have been crazy enough to load the thing," my husband said. We all milled around waiting for some kind of official announcement. No one was in the mood for a party anymore; that was for sure.

Four minutes later, Sheriff Croft mounted the steps and took the microphone. "Folks, I'm sorry to announce that the celebration is now officially over. If any of you saw or spoke to Roy Thompson within the last few hours, I'd appreciate it if you'd come forward so I could have a chat with you." As he said it, the sheriff looked directly at me. Did he think I'd killed the man just for taking a piece of cake? I knew it didn't look good that I'd argued with Roy so recently, but no one could believe that I'd take it in my mind to load that cannon with something that would hit Roy.

"Did the cannon kill him?" a voice from the crowd yelled out.

"I'm not here to answer your questions; I'm here to ask

them."

That didn't go over well with the crowd, and the sheriff knew it. He held up his hands as more folks clamored for information, until finally, Sheriff Croft said, "Settle down, folks. I can tell you that nothing was fired directly from the cannon. Roy was not hit with any flying projectiles, as far as we can tell."

"Did the sound of the explosion kill him, then? I understand he had a bad heart," someone else called out.

"As I said, that hasn't been determined at this time."

"Well, did the man die of natural causes, or did someone murder him?" another voice from nearby asked.

"We're not sure yet, but until we know for sure one way or the other, we're treating this as a crime scene of homicide. Now, that's the last question I'm going to ask. We've already got the area cordoned off, so if everyone will go to the barrier at Main Street, we'll take your names and contact information, and then you're free to go."

"We don't want to leave," someone shouted from the back. "We came all the way here to have a party."

The sheriff shook his head. "I don't know if it's had time to sink in yet, but a man died here, people. Show a little respect."

As he was leaving the stage, there were a few whispers, but no one else had the nerve to speak up. Why would anyone want to continue the party after what had just happened so publicly to Roy? I was the last person there who could be called a fan of the man, but I had no desire to go on with the festivities. I turned to Greg and said, "Well, it appears that the festival is over. Should we go back and open the diner early?"

"We can't," my husband said as he began to lead me toward the stage. "The sheriff wants to talk to us both, remember?"

"I don't know about you, but I really don't want to rehash what happened," I said. "It makes me sound so petty."

"Regardless, we don't have any choice. We don't want

Sheriff Croft coming to the diner looking for us later, do we?"

I visualized the sheriff driving up in his cruiser with the lights flashing and the siren wailing, but even though I knew that he most likely wouldn't do anything quite that dramatic, it did leave an indelible image in my mind. "No, you're right. Let's go. We might as well get this over with."

It wasn't that painless, though. There were quite a few people in front of us waiting to speak with the sheriff, and I wondered just how many people Roy Thompson had angered in Jasper Fork recently.

When it was finally our turn, the sheriff frowned at me as Greg and I approached. "I wondered if you two were going to come forward."

"I know that it's unfortunate that Roy and I had words earlier, but I was nowhere near him when he died. In fact, I was all the way across the square when the cannon went off. Did that firing have anything to do with him dying? Those poor old vets will never be able to forgive themselves if they ended up giving Roy a heart attack."

"I'll know more later," the sheriff said, "but you heard me before. I'm going on the assumption that whatever happened to Roy was done intentionally. Victoria, I heard that you threw the man out of the diner last night, and then you have an argument with him right in front of me not an hour before he died. What kind of vendetta did you have against him?"

"It wasn't anything that dire," I explained. "He came in last night, his usual cranky self, complaining about Jenny Hollister and the food she was serving him. I had finally had enough, so I threw him out. It's my right, after all."

The sheriff nodded as he jotted down the gist of our conversation in his ever present little notebook. "Greg, did you witness any of this?"

My husband nodded. "I wasn't about to miss it, to be honest with you. Sheriff, it was a long time coming, and everybody knows it."

"Who else was in the diner when it happened?" he asked.

I gave him a list of names, and he diligently wrote them all down.

"Now, about today," the sheriff said, quickly shifting gears.

"It was really just a continuation of our argument last night," I said. "I didn't want him to have that cake, and when I saw that plate in his hands, I just snapped." The moment I said it, I realized that my choice of words could have been better.

"What Victoria meant to say was that she just wanted to enforce her ban," Greg added, trying to do some damage control. "Honestly, she didn't snap at all. As a matter of fact, when we walked away from Roy in front of you, we didn't see him again until he died."

"Well, that's not exactly true," I said.

I didn't know which man looked more surprised by my statement, my husband or the sheriff. Greg spoke first. "You were with me the entire time, and we never got near him again."

"I didn't talk to him, but we *did* make eye contact across the square just before he died. He took a bite, and then he had the nerve to smile at me."

"What did you do?" the sheriff asked.

"Believe it or not, I just turned away."

"But you didn't say anything to him, is that correct?"

"That's correct," I said, echoing the sheriff's word choice.

"May we go now?" Greg asked.

"What's the rush?" the sheriff asked.

"Well, since the celebration is over now, we thought we might go ahead and open the diner back up. There's no reason in the world that we shouldn't, is there?"

"None that I can think of," the sheriff said. As we were walking away, he added, "You aren't planning on any trips out of town anytime soon, are you?"

"Why, are we suspects?" I asked as I turned back toward him.

"I'm just gathering information right now," he said.

"Then feel free to write this down," I said, a little louder than I needed to. "We didn't touch Roy Thompson, and we certainly didn't kill him."

"You didn't answer my question," the sheriff said, nonplussed by my declarative statement.

"We'll be at The Charming Moose, just like we are every day, for the foreseeable future," I said a little softer.

"Victoria, there's no way you're going to keep your nose out of this, is there?" the sheriff asked.

"What do you think?" I turned to reply, and then my husband and I left.

As Greg and I walked back to the diner, I asked my husband, "Is it possible that he really thinks we had something to do with Roy's death?"

"It's too soon to say," Greg said. "Can we blame him if he does? We *did* have a pretty public argument with the man."

"Don't try to sugarcoat it, Greg. *I* had the argument, and no one else."

"It could just as easily have been me," my sweet husband said. "Remember? If you hadn't stopped me, I'd be the one on the hot seat right now."

"But it wasn't you, was it?" I asked. "I'm just hoping that Roy dropped dead from a heart attack, and not something more ominous."

"I'm sure we all do, but why do you feel that way in particular?"

I shrugged as I explained, "If he died from foul play, I'm bound to be the first suspect on the sheriff's list, and if that's the case, Moose and I are going to have to solve another murder if we're going to keep me out of jail."

"Well, I have no desire to see you only once a week during visiting hours, so I suggest you and your grandfather go ahead and come up with a game plan, just in case. He'll help, won't he?"

"Are you kidding? He'll be chomping at the bit. You know how much he loves a good murder investigation."

"Even when his granddaughter is the main suspect in the case?"

"I'd have to believe that it only gives him more incentive," I said.

"Well, you can ask him yourself right now, because here he comes," Greg said. "I'm going to go ahead and get things ready to reopen. I'm sure the two of you have quite a few things you need to talk about. I love you," he said as he added a quick peck.

"I love you right back," I said, and then I turned to Moose. It meant the world to me to have Greg's support, but right now, I needed my grandfather's active assistance if I was going to prove that I didn't kill Roy Thompson, no matter how attractive that very act may have seemed in my daydreams the day before.

"Well, that's bad luck," Moose said as he met me. "Talk about bad timing."

"I know," I said. "Hey, if we're lucky, he died from natural causes and I don't have anything to worry about."

"I hate to be the one to convey bad news, but there's not a chance. Do you know Linda Taggart?"

"Not right off the top of my head. Why? Who is she?"

"She's a big shot forensic toxicologist teaching at UNC Asheville," he said. "Linda's a big fan of local celebrations, and we met a few years ago at Fire in the Mountains."

"The blacksmith festival in Spruce Pine?" I asked. "How did you happen to meet there?"

"We were watching a master blacksmith demonstrate how to make leaves out of iron, and we struck up a conversation. You know me. I seem to accumulate friends like some folks collect stamps or coins. Anyway, I was talking to her when Roy collapsed, and she offered the sheriff her services. He was game, so I managed to tag along when she examined Roy. It's not official yet, they'll have to run a battery of tests, but it's her opinion that someone poisoned Roy."

It was the worst news I could have gotten, and it must have shown on my face. "Moose, I'm in real trouble here."

"Why is that? Because The Charming Moose supplied the cake that probably killed him? Victoria, a dozen folks could have poisoned that piece after it left our hands and made its way into Roy's. Sure, it doesn't look good, but there are plenty enough other suspects so we shouldn't be the only ones under a cloud."

"Moose, you don't understand. I grabbed that cake from him right in front of the sheriff, and I had it ten seconds before he yanked it back. I could have easily poisoned the piece he was eating in the time I had it in my possession."

Moose nodded gravely. "I didn't realize that. I suppose that means that we'd better go ahead and get started."

"Then you'll help me investigate?" I asked.

"Trust me, granddaughter; nobody, and I mean nobody, had better try to stop me," he said, and I was happy yet again that Moose wasn't just my grandfather; he was one of my closest allies as well.

Chapter 3

"Should we go to Roy's office before the sheriff has a chance to visit it?" I asked. I knew that Roy Thompson kept a space not a hundred yards from where we were talking. I had no idea what he did all day, though. After all, since most of his holdings were in land, I wouldn't think that any of it would need much handling on a daily basis, but Roy was proud of his office.

"It's as good an idea as any," Moose said, so we walked in that direction. The facade of the building was done in weathered brick, and massive columns stood out front. As a matter of fact, they were a little too gaudy for my taste, but it was clear that pretension was important to Roy. As we walked through the massive oaken doors, I felt like whispering. It was that solemn a place.

That was lost the second we entered the building, though.

"A deal's a deal, and I'm not about to let him take advantage of me. Tell your boss that I'll see him in court before I let that happen!" James Manchester snapped as he nearly knocked us both over on his way out of the office. James occasionally ate at the diner, and he normally had a smile and a friendly word for me, but I doubted that he'd even recognized me he was so steamed at the moment. Mumbling a vague apology in our direction, James slammed the doors open and left.

"What put a bur under his saddle, do you suppose?" Moose asked me.

"I don't have a clue," I said as we approached Kelly Raven. Kelly was a dark-haired beauty a few years younger than I was, and while we'd never been friends, there had never been any reason for there to be any animosity between us.

At least not yet.

"Hi, Kelly. James was certainly in a huff, wasn't he?"

"It's not as bad as it must look to you. He and Mr. Thompson both have tempers, so the moment they became partners in their little venture, I knew I was in for trouble. From what Mr. Manchester said earlier, I was under the impression that you weren't exactly on good terms with my employer at the moment, either."

Kelly smiled brightly at us as she spoke, and I realized that no one had told her about her boss yet. Should Moose and I break it to her now, or instead, try to mine a little information first? I was still trying to decide when my grandfather decided to take matters into his own hands.

"We all have our moments," Moose said softly. "Has anyone been by to speak with you yet?"

She clearly didn't understand the nature of his question. "We've had a few folks stop in, but with the celebration, it's been rather quiet."

"I can't believe that no one told you," Moose said.

There was a hint of alarm in her eyes now. "Tell me what?"

"Roy died less than half an hour ago," I said, watching her carefully. I'd been hoping for some kind of reaction, but all she did was look at me to see if I was joking.

"I'm afraid it's true," Moose said. "He's gone."

The news finally started to sink in, and Kelly pulled a tissue from her drawer and held it to her chest. "Was it his heart?"

"Why, was he having problems with his health?" I asked.

"No, but for a man his age, it's a logical question, isn't it?"

"I suppose so," I said. I took a deep breath of air, and then I explained, "He was poisoned, as a matter of fact. Do you have any idea who might want to see him dead?"

"Poison? Really?" I was waiting for her to ask how he'd been dosed, and I wasn't exactly sure how I was going to tap dance around that particular answer, but it turned out that I didn't have to.

Moose said, "It really could help if you knew of anyone."

Kelly sat back in her chair, looking stunned, and not much like the lovely woman she'd seemed to be earlier. This was more a little girl, afraid, and more than a little confused. "I just don't know. I don't have to tell either one of you that Mr. Thompson wasn't the easiest person in the world to get along with. I've worked for him for seven years, and there have been times I've wanted to walk out that door in a huff myself. That's a horrid thing to admit right now, isn't it?"

She began to cry softly, and Moose laid a hand on her shoulder. She seemed to take a great deal of comfort from his act of kindness and compassion, and I wondered yet again how my grandfather could do what he did with just a single touch. He was amazing when it came to offering comfort, and when he tried to ease someone's pain, he nearly always succeeded.

"There, there," he said softly, and after a moment, she nodded, wiped at her eyes carefully, and then gathered herself again.

"If anyone poisoned him, I would think it would probably be his ex-wife, Sylvia Jones. She lives in Molly's Corners. Frankly, she hated Mr. Thompson, and she wasn't a bit shy about who knew it. I don't know how that pair managed to stay married as long as they did before they finally divorced. The only times I ever saw them together, they acted as though they wanted to kill each other." She must have realized how that sounded, because she quickly went on. "Mr. Thompson's son was no better." She shivered a little in her chair, as if the very thought of the younger man scared her. "Asher didn't come here often, but when he did, I always felt as though he was staring at me and thinking vile thoughts." Kelly paused, and then added with a slight smile, "I know that I sound a tad melodramatic, but I can't help it. There's no other way to describe it."

"Is there anyone else you can think of?" Moose asked in his gentlest voice.

"There's someone, but I don't know exactly who it is.

Mr. Thompson had a heated telephone conversation with a new partner, and he was as angry as I've ever seen him. I just wish I knew who it was. And then there was his stalker."

"Stalker? Someone was following him around?" I asked.

"He thought it was some kind of joke at first," Kelly said. "He'd turn around, and she'd duck out of sight like a chipmunk running for cover. I'm sorry, but I don't know who she was, either."

"Don't worry. We can ask around," I said.

Kelly nodded, and then she looked at me curiously. "Excuse me for asking, but why exactly are you both so interested in what happened to Mr. Thompson? I never realized you'd ever consider him a friend, and I know it's not because he was a customer at your diner. He seemed to take a great deal of pleasure in crowing about his complaints concerning your food."

We were saved from answering her question when the doors opened again. I half expected to see James Manchester reenter, but instead, it was Sheriff Croft, and from the sour expression on his face, it was clear that he wasn't at all pleased about finding us in Roy Thompson's office ahead of him.

As he approached, he asked us, "How long have you two been here?"

"Not long at all," I said quickly.

The sheriff shook his head. "I don't like it, not one little bit. You had to know I was headed this way next."

"We didn't mean anything by it," I replied quickly. "We just wanted to be sure that someone told Kelly about what happened."

"Frankly, I'm surprised that you'd be all that eager for her to know what happened to her boss," the sheriff said.

"Why would you say that?" Kelly asked, clearly confused by the sheriff's comment.

"They didn't tell you, did they?" he asked as he glanced over at her.

"Tell me what?"

"It was their celebration cake that did your boss in."

Kelly couldn't have looked more surprised if the sheriff had told her that we were the town's new royal family. "I don't understand," she said. "Why would either one of them want to kill him?"

"We didn't," I said hastily. "But you can see why we'd want to find out who did."

"That's enough, you two," the sheriff said. "I'll be by the diner for a little chat in a bit, but for now, I'd appreciate it if you'd both head back there and stay until I get around to it. Agreed?"

"Yes, sir," I said aloud, though Moose only nodded.

"Good bye, Kelly," I said as we were leaving, but she didn't reply. While I felt a little bad about taking advantage of her, we were investigating her boss's murder, so I thought that gave us a little leeway in trying to get information from her.

As Moose and I walked back to the diner, I had to wonder which one of his enemies might have poisoned Roy Thompson. Whoever had done it had made a critical mistake using our cake to kill him. Now it directly involved me and my family, and we'd relentlessly search until we found the killer ourselves, if the police didn't manage to catch them first.

"So, who should we talk to first?" Moose asked me after we left the office. "Manchester looked pretty steamed. I personally think we should track him down while he's still upset. Who knows? Maybe we'll get lucky."

I looked at my grandfather to see if he was teasing me, but he looked deadly serious. "Moose, you *did* hear the sheriff, right? We're under orders to go straight back to the diner and wait for him. It was pretty clear that he was not very happy with us."

"We both know that he's going to be tied up with Kelly for at least an hour. That gives us plenty of time to track James Manchester down first before he comes looking for us."

I grabbed my grandfather's arm and stopped him. "If we do that, Sheriff Croft is going to hear about it, and we both know it. We can't take a chance of getting on his bad side. I know how hard it is to do this, but at least this time, we need to do as we're told."

Moose frowned and pursed his lips for a second before speaking. "I guess you're right, but I hate to let an opportunity pass like that. If we wait too long, Manchester's going to have time to collect himself."

"We really don't have much choice."

"I know you're right, but I don't have to like it," Moose said. My grandfather was a real go-getter, and to be honest, I was much the same way, but there were times when one of us had to put on the brakes, or we'd constantly be getting ourselves into all kinds of trouble.

Back at the diner, we found the place brimming with people. Ellen was swamped with customers, even though Martha, my grandmother, was helping out as well. "What's going on?" I asked her.

"With the celebration canceled so abruptly, folks didn't have anywhere else to go. Most of the street vendors have already packed up and left." She kissed Moose soundly, and then she said, "It might not be a bad thing if you lend Greg a hand in the kitchen. I called Melinda, but I couldn't reach her."

My mother, who normally worked the grill as our morning cook, was on her way to the mountains with my father for the day.

"It doesn't surprise me. She left her cell phone at home," I said.

"Should we go try to find her?" Martha asked.

I just smiled. "It wasn't done by accident. Mom and Dad wanted to get away for the day. They'll be back before dark, but in the meantime, we can handle this ourselves."

"Of course we can," Moose said as he literally rolled up

his sleeves. "I'm happy to help out in the kitchen. It will be just like old times."

I grabbed a pitcher filled with iced sweet tea in one hand, and then added a coffee pot to the other as I started topping off glasses and cups.

An hour later, I was ringing up a party of eight when I felt a tap on my shoulder. "Give me one second," I said without even turning around.

"I don't have that much time," a familiar voice said.

I looked at the sheriff and said, "Sorry, but I can't help you, then. As you can see, we're jammed at the moment, but if you can come back in five minutes, I should have some time to talk to you."

"I might as well eat while I'm waiting," he said as he started for an empty stool at the counter. "Come over and join me when you get a breather."

I nodded as I finished ringing up the orders in my hand. I saw Martha greet the sheriff, so I knew that he was well taken care of as I finished up with the last of the customers in line. We had a bit of a lull at the register, so I made my way over to the sheriff.

"What can I do for you?"

He took a sip of tea, and then put the glass down. "I need to know what Kelly Raven said to you earlier."

I glanced at the clock over the counter. "You were there for over an hour. I can't believe she said anything to us that she didn't tell you."

"Well, I won't know that until you tell me about your conversation, will I?"

"Are you being snippy with me, Sheriff?"

He frowned down at his tea, though I knew that his displeasure was with Moose and me. "Victoria, you and your grandfather headed straight to Roy Thompson's office as soon as we finished talking, and what was even worse, you did it behind my back."

"Hang on a second," I said. "The man had a piece of cake from our diner, and then he died. You knew we were

going to investigate what happened, you as much as said so
yourself. Why are you so surprised that we'd start digging
immediately?"

"I'm not, but I didn't expect you to jump ahead of me
like that."

"You know that we always do our best to stay out of your
way," I said, "but this is personal, and you know it. I
apologize if we stepped on your toes, but what choice did we
have?"

"You could just let me handle this," he said. In a gentler
voice, he asked, "Victoria, don't you think I know how to do
my job?"

The man's feelings were hurt, that much was clear. I
didn't always think about the ramifications of what Moose
and I did, and we'd all managed to be friends for years before
Moose and I started getting dragged into murder. It was
clearly time to do a little damage control with our
relationship. "Sheriff, we know you're good at what you do.
It's just that there are times when folks will tell us things that
they'll automatically keep from you. It's just human nature.
And remember, we always tell you what we discover as soon
as we can. My grandfather and I would never do anything to
undermine your authority, or try to hamper your
investigations."

"It's easier to *say* that you're not going to do something
than it is to actually refrain from doing it," he said, though he
seemed a little placated.

Everything would have been just fine if Moose hadn't
been eavesdropping via the pass-through window. "My
granddaughter said what she meant, Sheriff."

"How long have you been listening to our conversation?"
Sheriff Croft asked.

"It's my diner. I can eavesdrop whenever I want to," he
said loudly.

I hated to do it, but I had to spank my grandfather a little,
or we were going to lose the tenuous amount of goodwill I'd
just gained with our local law enforcement. "Funny, I

thought that *I* owned the place these days, Moose, or am I mistaken?"

He waved a hand in the air. "Sure, technically it belongs to you, but that's beside the point. Blast it all, I'm trying to defend you here, girl."

"Moose, I haven't been a girl in quite a while, something we're both well aware of, and when exactly did I need *anyone* to defend me?"

My grandfather looked exasperated by my reaction, but I noticed that the sheriff's scowl had eased up quite a bit. Moose turned to Greg, and though I couldn't see my husband directly, I knew that he was manning the grill. "Help me out here, Greg."

I could hear my husband chuckle from where I sat. "Sorry, but you're on your own with this one."

Moose shook his head. "Who would have believed it? My own family's turning on me."

Martha approached the window, and my grandfather turned to her. "Surely my own wife has my back here."

She reached through and patted his cheek as she smiled. "Not this time, Dear. Now, don't you have some mooseburgers to make? Try as he might, Greg still hasn't mastered your technique, and as soon as folks heard you were working the grill with him, they started ordering them like crazy." My grandmother paused, and then she turned to Greg. "I meant no offense to you. You're a fine cook in your own right."

"Hey, I don't disagree with them. I like Moose's version better than mine myself."

It rarely happened, but my grandfather was clearly flummoxed by our behavior. "You've all gone over the edge; you know that, don't you?"

"Whatever you say, Dear," Martha said, and I watched as my grandfather's countenance softened. I might have been the bravest person in the family when it came to standing up to my grandfather when he needed to be brought in check, but my grandmother could win a smile with just a glance, even when he was at his crabbiest. "Now, those mooseburgers aren't going to make themselves, are they?"

"I'll get right on it," Moose said. "At least I understand *that* part of my life."

I turned back to the sheriff, and his smile was open and warm now. "That was quite a show. I hope it wasn't all on my account."

"Don't give yourself too much credit," I said with a smile. "Moose needs to be reminded every now and then who's really in charge around here these days, and I'm more than happy to do it."

"You're braver than most men in the county," the sheriff said.

"Aw, he's just a pussycat if you dig down deep enough."

"Sorry, but my shovel doesn't reach down that far," the sheriff said.

Moose slid a plate through the window. "Number twelve is ready."

I grabbed the sheriff's plate—fried chicken, fried okra, and a biscuit—and slid it in front of him.

He studied it for a moment, and then he asked with a smile, "Do you think it's safe for me to eat this?"

"Moose takes his food seriously," I said. "He might browbeat you halfway down the street, but he would never serve anything he wouldn't be willing to eat himself. If you don't believe me, ask him yourself."

"No, I trust you both," he said, and then he picked up the chicken and took a healthy bite. "Man, this is some kind of wonderful."

"We're glad you like it," I said. I knew that I'd have to smooth things over with my grandfather later, but at least I'd managed to keep the sheriff from locking us both up for obstructing justice.

"Now, about Kelly Raven," he said as he stabbed a few pieces of fried okra and waved them in the air. "What exactly did she tell you?"

I glanced at the register before I answered and saw a few

people standing in line waiting for me. "Tell you what. You finish eating, and then we'll talk."

"Promise?" the sheriff asked. "What if you get busy again?"

"Martha will take over the register, and Greg can handle the kitchen by himself. Moose and I will make ourselves available to you, no matter what."

"That's all I can ask," he said as he took a bite of his biscuit. The look of sheer pleasure on his face was worth watching.

I rang up the customers, and then I walked back into the kitchen. Greg smiled at me, but Moose had nothing but a scowl for me.

I took a deep breath, and then I said, "Before you say one word, tell me that I wasn't right."

"About which part?" Moose asked sullenly.

"About every part," I answered. "It's my diner now, right?"

"Right," he replied grudgingly.

"Right?" I asked. "Try to say it this time with a little more enthusiasm."

"Right," Moose said a little more brightly.

"And I can take care of myself, can't I?" I asked.

He stared at me, and then he started laughing. "I can't very well deny it, can I?" He turned to Greg and asked, "How do you do it?"

"Do what?"

"Get along so well with this stubborn, strong minded, opinionated, independent woman?"

Greg just laughed. "Go ask Martha about being married to someone with those exact same qualities. I'm willing to bet that her answer will be the same as mine. We happen to love the people we're married to, *because* of who they are, not in spite of it."

"I'm not *all* of those things," Moose said.

I couldn't help laughing.

Moose studied me for a few seconds, and then he asked,

"What's so funny, Victoria?"

"Not a thing in the world," I said as I reached up and kissed his cheek. "You're one of a kind. You know that, don't you?"

"I'm not sure that you can say that so emphatically. You and I seem to have quite a few things in common."

I grinned at him. "I'm taking that as a compliment. You know that, don't you?"

"Why wouldn't you? I happen to think that you're just about perfect."

"You're just biased because you're my grandfather," I replied.

"I certainly hope so," Moose said. He glanced out the window, and then added, "Sheriff Sourpuss is just about finished with his meal. I suppose we'll have to talk to him before long."

"There's no time like the present," I said.

"I don't guess we have much choice," Moose replied. "Lead on."

"We're ready if you are," I told the sheriff as Moose and I approached him. "There's a table free over by the window we can grab." I hated leaving Martha and Ellen to wait tables and run the register, but hopefully it wouldn't be for long. At least things were slowing down enough for us to have a few minutes. I found myself wishing that it would just take that long, but I wasn't about to hold my breath.

As we got settled in, the sheriff pulled out his ever-present notebook and pen, and then he looked at us. "Let's get started. First things first. Tell me everything that happened from the moment you walked in that building."

"Actually, it sort of started before we even made it inside," I replied.

The sheriff sighed for a second, and then he said, "That's fine. Start wherever you need to. Just don't leave anything out."

Chapter 4

"Are you sure that's it?" the sheriff asked as he finished taking the last note. Between the two of us, my grandfather and I had relayed every word and expression that we'd heard and seen in Roy Thompson's office during our conversation with Kelly.

"Every last thing that we heard," Moose said.

"Good," the sheriff said as he stopped writing and closed up his notebook. "I appreciate your cooperation."

"That works both ways, doesn't it, Sheriff?" Moose asked.

"What do you mean?"

I explained, "Well, we were pretty forthcoming with you. Can you at least return the favor? What did you find out so far that we don't know?"

Sheriff Croft shook his head. "I shouldn't have to remind either one of you that it doesn't work that way. I wouldn't even be here right now if you two hadn't gotten to Kelly Raven before I could manage it myself."

Moose waved a hand in the air. "That's old business, Sheriff; we've been properly scolded already. Surely you can give us something. How else are we going to stay out of your way if we don't know where you're headed?"

He thought about it for five seconds before he spoke. "I'm still collecting information, and I really don't have much more than what you two got out of Kelly. I will say this. Her story is remarkably consistent in the retelling, from what she told us."

"Was it to the point where it sounded memorized, or was there enough variation that it sounded believable?" I asked.

"I don't know. She seemed to hit the same highlights with you as she did with me, but unless I knew exactly what she told you word for word, there's no way to know. You didn't happen to record your conversation with her, did you?"

"We'd never do that," I said.

"Just because we never thought of it before, but we're going tape recorder shopping as soon as you leave," my grandfather said.

I wasn't sure if Moose was kidding or not, and clearly, neither was the sheriff. "I would advise strongly against doing that, Moose."

"Why? It could be very helpful at some point."

"Don't overestimate its value. We have recordings we take that accompany signed statements that the subject volunteered for the interview, and they still get thrown out on technicalities sometimes. You're just asking for trouble if you try it, and there's no real upside to the risk you'd be taking."

"Don't worry. We're not going to do it." I turned to my grandfather and asked, "Right, Moose?"

"Hey, it was just a thought. Don't worry. I've already forgotten it."

The sheriff nodded, and then he said, "Now, if you two will excuse me, I've got some suspects to interview."

"Who are you going to start with first?" Moose asked, clearly eager to get started with our own investigation.

"Do we honestly have to have this conversation again so soon? At least for now, I want you both to stay away from James Manchester, Sylvia Jones, and her son, Asher. Do we understand each other?"

"How long is 'for now'?" I asked him. "Six hours? Eight?"

"What? No. Days. I'm talking days."

"Well, we both know that's not going to happen, so there's no use pretending that it is," Moose said, and for once, I kept my mouth shut. I happened to agree with him. If the sheriff tried to take every suspect away from us, we'd be left out in the cold, and the threat to our diner's reputation wouldn't allow us to sit idly by and trust the sheriff to clear our good family name.

The sheriff wasn't all that happy with us, but I agreed with my grandfather. This was not the time to back down. "How about two days, then?" he suggested.

"We'll stay away until tomorrow morning," Moose countered.

"Noon tomorrow, and that's my final offer."

Moose frowned, glanced at me, and then he saw me nod. In an instant, he stuck out his hand. "Sold. It's a pleasure doing business with you, Sheriff."

Sheriff Croft looked bemused as he took my grandfather's hand and shook it. "I have a hunch my life would be a whole lot easier if I just locked you both up and forgot where I put the key."

"We all know that you'd never do that, no matter how tempted you might be," I said with a grin as the front door opened, "but if you ever decide to, Rebecca will have us out in a heartbeat, and nobody will be happy after that."

"Did someone just mention my name?" my best friend asked as she walked into the diner.

"Speak of the devil, and he appears," Moose said with a grin.

"Actually, *she* appears," Rebecca said with a grin. "Was there something I could do for you, Sheriff?"

"I was just leaving, counselor," he said, and did as he promised.

After the sheriff was gone, Rebecca asked, "What was that all about? Or do I really want to know?"

"Sometimes ignorance is bliss," I said. "It's nice to see you. To what do we owe the pleasure?"

"What do you mean?" she asked. "I'm here all the time."

"Not that often," I corrected her, "and rarely in the afternoon."

"What can I say?" she asked with a smile. "I just felt like playing a little hooky. Care to join me, or are you too busy with your murder investigation?"

"How did you know we were investigating Roy

Thompson's murder?"

"Come on. He died eating a slice of your cake. Why wouldn't you dig into it? Was that why the sheriff was here? Did he tell you to stay out of it?"

"He did, but just for twenty-one hours," I said.

"Then you have time for a little shopping," Rebecca said.

I looked at Moose. "What do you think? We don't have much to go on without those three suspects. I can spare an hour, can't I? My next shift here doesn't technically start until five."

"Go," he said agreeably, something that instantly got my suspicions up.

"Moose, you're not going to do anything foolish like investigate on your own without me, are you? We promised the sheriff, remember?"

"If memory serves, we agreed to stay away from three specific suspects. Knowing Roy Thompson, I'm willing to wager that there were more folks than that who wouldn't mind seeing the man dead."

I turned to Rebecca. "Sorry, but I can't go. I have to babysit my grandfather."

"I understand," she said as she started to stand.

Moose said angrily, "Nobody, and I mean nobody, needs to babysit me."

"Then promise me you'll stay here, or I'm not going anywhere."

Moose mulled that over, and then finally, he said, "How about if I make a few telephone calls from the office in back? That would keep me here. Would that make you happy?"

"More than I can express," I said as I kissed his cheek, and then I turned to Rebecca. "Let's go. I'm all yours."

I waved happily to my grandfather as we walked out, and after a moment, he smiled and waved back to me. I had no doubt that he'd make productive use of the time I was gone, but I needed to relax a little with Rebecca. We spent far too little time together these days, and I found myself missing her.

It was just too bad that murder had a way of getting between us.

By the time I got back to the diner, I was feeling much better. Spending time with Rebecca always seemed to do that to me. She was one of those old friends that, no matter how long the gap between our visits, it was as though no time at all had passed between us when we managed to get together again. The feelings of happiness I was experiencing didn't last all that long, though. My grandfather was waiting impatiently for me by the front door when I walked in, ready and eager to go. I just hoped he had a lead worth following that didn't include the list of suspects that the sheriff was currently pursuing.

"Come on, Victoria. Let's go," Moose said as he clutched his coat in his hands. "I've been on the phone since you left, and I'm getting some real gold from my contacts."

"He wanted to call you a dozen times, but I wouldn't let him," Martha said calmly after she finished ringing up one of our customers.

"She's worse than you sometimes," Moose said with a hint of ire in his voice. If there was one person around who could control my grandfather besides me, it was his wife, not that I thought I could ever manipulate Moose into doing something that he didn't want to do. The man could be so stubborn at times that it was a job convincing him that a plan had been his in the first place.

"I told you it wouldn't kill you to wait," Martha said with a soft smile.

"Okay, I didn't die from it, but it pretty near knocked me unconscious. Now, are we going to stand here all afternoon gabbing, Victoria, or are we going to go follow up on my new leads?"

"I'm ready to go wherever you lead me," I said.

"Then the first place we're going is out of this diner."

"Don't I at least have a second to say hello to my husband?" I asked as I spotted Greg through the order window.

I waved, and he returned the gesture as he said, "Go on. He's been driving us all crazy ever since you left. You'll be doing us all a favor if you go with him wherever the man's headed."

"I'd resent that remark if it didn't serve my purposes," Moose told Greg.

"That's about what I figured, or I wouldn't have said it in the first place," my good-natured husband answered with a big grin. It took a lot to rile him up, and I'd only seen it a few times since we'd been married, but it was something that I was in no hurry to witness again. My husband, level-headed and easygoing, could be pushed to the point where he struck back, but it took a lot to do it. Once it did, though, I pitied the person who mistook his calm demeanor for someone who was a pushover.

"Come on, then. Let's go," I said.

As we got outside and started walking toward Moose's truck, I asked, "Where exactly are we going, or is it a secret?"

"No secrets between us," Moose said. As he opened the passenger side truck door for me, he grinned. "Did you know that Roy Thompson was seeing someone on the sly?"

"You don't mean romantically, do you?" I asked, aghast by the claim.

Moose looked at me carefully. "Why does that surprise you, because of his age?"

"Heavens, no. I've been at the diner too long not to realize that men of any age can be fools for love. I just can't imagine anyone loving that old sourpuss back."

Moose grinned. "I'll give you that one. If you think that's something, wait until you hear who it was."

He'd pulled out of the parking lot, and I knew the general direction we were going on. I tried to think of any women in town who might be able to stand Roy, but I drew a total blank.

Then we pulled up in front of Chris's Barbershop.

"You're kidding me," I said as I looked through the painted window inside to see three women, spaced from their thirties to their sixties, all cutting hair. Most folks seemed surprised to find an old fashioned barbershop just off Main Street with three women working the clippers, but for me, it was all that I'd ever known. In my opinion, it was odd to think of barbershops being run by men.

"It's not Chris, is it?" I asked. She ran the place, and had Casey and Taylor cutting with her. Was it just a coincidence that all three women had names that could have just as easily been men? It had to be, but I didn't want to try to figure the odds.

"It is, indeed. Why do you ask?"

"Well, Casey's too young for him, at least I hope she is, and Taylor tends to like her men on the younger side, if what I've seen in the diner is any indication. I don't know. I always figured that Chris was too smart to be hoodwinked by a man like Roy Thompson."

"Granddaughter, not everyone saw the same man you did when they looked at Roy. I know what a pain he was at the diner, but he could also be charming when it suited him."

"I don't like this," I told Moose. "How are we going to broach the subject with her? It's not exactly common knowledge that they'd been dating, or I would have heard about it. I'm not so sure she'd appreciate us outing her like that."

"My, don't you have a high opinion of your knowledge of our little town," Moose said with a smile.

"Hey, you didn't know, either," I protested.

"That's a good point."

"So, I'm curious," I asked as we got out of his truck. "Who was your source?"

"I may not work for the newspaper, but I still can't reveal it," Moose said solemnly.

"Not even to your partner?" I asked.

"I was asked to keep it quiet, and I'm going to keep my word."

"That's all I needed to hear," I said. Keeping your word was a big deal in my family, and we've been known to lose opportunities to make some good money in the short term when someone violated their bond. Some tried to make it up to us, giving in and claiming that they meant what they'd said all along, but they were always met with resounding silence. If you couldn't trust someone to keep their word on a handshake and a promise, there was no contract ever written that could make any of us ever enter into a deal again with anyone who had lied to us in the first place.

"Should I tackle her by myself, or do you want in on it, too?" I asked Moose.

"Just wait out here, Victoria," he said.

"Not a chance," I replied with a grin. "You're not getting rid of me that easily."

"I'm not trying to lock you out of this," Moose said impatiently. "I'm going to ask Chris to come outside and talk to us, and I'm going to present it so that she thinks you've got something to ask her in private, which is true."

Chris noticed us standing out front, and she waved tentatively in our direction with her clippers. She was a slim, older woman, with closely cropped hair that was halfway through the transition from brown to silver.

"Why me?" I asked as I waved back, doing my best not to smile at her. I didn't want Chris to think we were there for haircuts.

"If I go in and ask her alone, there's a better chance that she'll come outside to talk to you," Moose said, and before I could refute it, he walked into the barbershop. I had no choice but to back his play, knowing that I could trust him to do what he'd said he would do.

Sure enough, Chris came out immediately, despite the older man still sitting in her chair. She said something to him as he started to get up, but he settled back into the chair quickly enough.

Chris came out on Moose's heels. "Victoria, what's so urgent, and why couldn't we discuss this inside? Kyle

Norman's not too happy with either one of us right now."

"Kyle has nowhere else to be, and we all know it," Moose said.

Chris just waved off his comment, her gaze never leaving me. "I'm waiting, Victoria."

I took a deep gulp of air, and said, "Moose and I didn't want anyone else inside to know that you've been dating Roy Thompson."

As I said it, all the blood went out of her face, and if Moose hadn't been standing nearby to steady her, I have no doubt that she would have hit the sidewalk in front of her shop like a big bag of sand.

"Are you okay?" Moose asked Chris as he helped her to the bench in front of the barbershop. In warmer weather, it was a magnet for the old men in town to sit around and gossip, but thankfully, it was a little too chilly for that today.

"I'm fine. I don't know why I reacted like that. I wasn't ashamed of going out with Roy, but I thought we'd been pretty cagey about keeping it quiet. How'd you find out?"

Moose was about to answer when I said, "Our source asked for our discretion, and we're going to give it. Chris, if word gets out, it won't be from us. Moose and I are digging into what happened to Roy, though, and we'd appreciate any help you could give us."

"I wish I could," she said with a frown, "but you see, Roy and I broke up last week. I suppose that there was a chance that we might get back together later, but somebody sure stole that from us, didn't they?"

"Why did you break up, if you don't mind us asking?" I asked gently.

"There was no major rift, if that's what you're trying to figure out. Roy and I just decided to go our separate ways for the moment. I kissed him on the cheek good bye, and that was that. Sorry I can't give you a more explosive story, but there was no hate there, or love either, truth be told. We might have found it later if we'd had more time, but it wasn't there yet. Why are you two so interested in my love life all of a sudden?"

I was about to answer when she held up one hand. "Strike that. It makes sense. He was poisoned with your cake. Why wouldn't you try to solve his murder? I'm just sorry I can't help. Now, if you'll excuse me, I have to get back to Kyle's haircut. As it is, the old miser's probably going to try to get a reduced price because he had to wait."

"Chris, were you at the celebration earlier?" I asked her.

She turned, stared at me for a second, and then she said, "My chair was never empty. I couldn't afford to close the place. I was here from eight this morning, and the first time I've stepped out the door was to talk to you. You can ask my girls, or any of the customers I cut. Now, is that all?"

"That's it. I hope there are no hard feelings," I said.

"Not between us," she said with a slight grin. "Good luck with your hunt."

"Thanks. We'll need it."

After Chris walked back in and picked her scissors up, I asked Moose, "Do you believe her story?"

"About the breakup? It sounds about right. The only thing is that she didn't seem all that choked up that someone killed Roy, did she?"

I shook my head. "If they'd broken up six months ago, her reaction would have been perfect, but since it was just last week, by her own words, she was a little too casual about the whole thing."

"She's got an alibi, though," Moose said. "Nobody would make that bold a claim without being able to back it up."

"You're not worried that her employees might lie to protect her?" I asked.

"Not about murder. As far as I'm concerned, she's in the clear unless we learn something that contradicts what she just told us. Are you ready for a little ride?"

"Sure, I'm up for it if you are. Where are we going?"

"Our next lead is in Molly's Corners," he said.

The town was a good half hour away from ours, and I

wondered who we'd be visiting. "Who are we going to be talking to there?"

"It turns out that James Manchester wasn't the only business partner Roy crossed. He also had some pretty bad blood recently with Hank Mullins."

"Hang on a second. He's the mayor there, right?"

"He is," Moose affirmed. "Apparently Roy only partnered with folks rich enough to afford losing their investments with him."

"Didn't anyone ever *make* any money working with him?" I asked as Moose drove to the next town.

"I'm sure that they did, but earning money isn't much of an incentive to kill someone, is it? I figure the only folks who had cause to want to see Roy dead lost something in their bargains with him."

"You realize that we could be in for a long list of names before this is all over, don't you?" I asked.

"That's why it's so important we get busy now," Moose said.

"I can't argue with that."

Chapter 5

"How exactly are we going to approach Hank Mullins?" I asked as Moose and I drove to Molly's Corners. "We can't exactly say, 'Hi there, Mr. Mayor. You didn't happen to kill Roy Thompson, did you?' It wouldn't make us his most popular visitors of the day, would it?"

"You'd be surprised. I've got a hunch that being mayor has its own set of troubles, but no, we're not going into this cold. I've got a message from someone he's bound to listen to. He might not like talking to us, but he can't afford to say no when he knows who's on our side."

"Wow, we sound important all of a sudden," I said with a smile. "Who is this backer whose name we're about to drop?"

He mumbled something in response, but even sitting as close to him as I was on the bench seat of his truck, I still couldn't hear the name. "Care to repeat that in a decibel level above where termites talk?"

"It's Holly Dixon," Moose admitted grudgingly.

"You called the judge for a favor, knowing how your wife feels about the woman? You've got some nerve, that's all I can say."

"Victoria," he replied heatedly, "Martha has no reason to be jealous of Holly. I've told her that until I'm blue in the face, but she just won't listen to me."

"She might have a little reason," I said, remembering the last time I'd seen my grandfather and the judge in the same room. They'd been like two teenagers with a secret that no one else was in on. It made me suspicious of their past, and I didn't even have a dog in the fight. I wasn't at all surprised that Martha had never warmed up to the woman.

"That's nonsense," he said dismissively, but I wasn't about to let it go that easily.

"It's not nonsense if your wife feels otherwise," I said. "Moose, we don't have to solve this murder that badly. I don't want you getting in trouble with your wife over it."

"Holly and I are just friends. There's no reason I shouldn't have called her, and there's nothing I feel guilty about. Now, I've just about said all I'm going to on the subject. Do we understand each other?"

I knew that tone of voice; it was time to drop it, at least for now. "Got it." I looked out the window at the barren trees as we passed through the mountains. "I miss the leaves; I can't wait until they show up again."

"You do tend to jump around sometimes when you talk, don't you?" he asked with amusement thick in his voice.

"Hey, I'm nothing if not an obedient granddaughter," I said.

We both held it as long as we could, and then my grandfather and I both burst out laughing at nearly the same time.

As we drove into Molly's Corners, I found myself enjoying the architecture of the town. It was different enough from Jasper Fork, and yet similar enough to make me feel as though I was in a place of odd familiarity. The town square was different, though. While ours was an actual square, theirs was much more of a long rectangle, and while we had a cannon in the center of ours, they had a large L constructed of fine white stone, built in honor of the original Molly, at least the one the town had been named after. Molly had been one of the first settlers in the area, and their group had been at war with a local tribe of Catawbas. Molly's husband died defending their land, and without hesitation, history said that Molly held out until darkness came, and then she slipped away into a nearby creek with her daughter. They managed to make their way back to the nearest settlement, ten miles away on foot, traveling only at night, and when she'd been asked how they'd managed it, Molly had said she just peeked around every corner until no one was there. I kind of liked the name of the town myself.

As Moose parked, he asked me, "So, are you ready for this?"

"I'm going to follow your lead this time," I said. "After all, you're the one with the letter of recommendation."

"I don't have a letter," he told me. "Holly just told me that I could use her name if I thought it might help."

"I understood that. I meant what I said, though. I'll let you take the lead."

"That would be great."

We walked into the town hall, and Moose approached a police officer standing nearby. "We're looking for the mayor."

The officer looked us over, and then he pointed to a nearby door. As we started toward it, he said in a voice barely above a whisper to me, "If your business can wait, you might want to come back tomorrow. He's already thrown three people out of his office today."

"Is that some kind of record?" I asked, just as softly. I stayed behind, and Moose hadn't even realized that I'd tarried.

"Are you kidding? We're not even close yet, but I have a hunch we're about to add two more names to the list."

"Thanks for the heads-up, but we'll take our chances," I said.

Moose finally noticed my absence. He paused, turned around, and then he asked me, "Victoria, are you coming?"

"Don't say I didn't warn you," the cop said with a smile. "See you in a second."

"We'll see," I replied.

I caught up with Moose, and as I did, he asked, "What was that all about?"

"It appears that the mayor is in one bad mood."

"Well, it's not getting better for him any time soon," Moose said.

If we weren't investigating a murder, I would have looked forward to the confrontation that was about to happen.

My grandfather was quite good at arguing his way around any issue, and it sounded as though the mayor was a man cut from the same cloth.

There was a stylish woman in her sixties sitting behind the desk when we walked through the door, and I noticed that she perked up considerably the second she laid eyes on my grandfather. "How may I help you?" she asked. The name 'Helen Parsons' was etched on her nameplate, and it was placed precisely on her desk.

How had the old charmer managed such intense and immediate attention? I didn't blame my grandmother one bit for resenting the attention that Moose got at times from women his age, and even younger.

"Helen, it's so nice to meet you. We're here to see Hank," Moose said in an easy voice that made it sound as though he and the mayor were old friends. It was bold, a big fat lie, and told very convincingly.

The woman smiled at the sound of her name, but it dimmed when Moose mentioned the name Hank. In a soft voice, she said, "No one calls him Hank here. It's Mr. Mayor, or Mayor Mullins. Anything else gets you thrown out immediately."

Moose smiled warmly at her. "Thank you for the tip. Would it be possible for us to see him?"

"May I ask what it is in reference to?" she asked, her smile warming right back up. Honestly, it was as though I wasn't even there.

"I'd tell you if I could, but I'm afraid it's rather personal," Moose said lazily.

"I don't doubt it, but if I try to send someone into his office without giving the mayor fair notice about what it is concerning, I'll lose my job. I'm truly sorry, but there's nothing I can do about it."

"We completely understand," Moose said. "I'm sure he wouldn't want us broadcasting it, but we'd like to talk to him about his connection to Roy Thompson, the man who was murdered in Jasper Fork earlier today."

That got an immediate reaction. Ms. Parsons stood abruptly, slipped past us, and went to the door across the way from her. She entered without knocking, or sparing us a single look back.

"Wow, *that* turned out to be a hot button, didn't it?" I asked Moose.

"I believe that we hit a nerve," my grandfather said.

"While we have a second, I have a question for you. Do you realize it when you're doing it, or does it just come naturally to you?"

Moose was still staring at the door Ms. Parsons had walked through, and he barely gave my question a second thought. "Do what?"

"Seduce every woman anywhere near your age that you come into contact with," I said.

That got his attention. "I'll have you know that I've been loyal to your grandmother since the day we said our vows, young lady."

"Okay, maybe 'seduce' was the wrong word. How about charm? Do you like that any better? You should, since it's what you named your diner when you opened up. Sometimes I forget just how slick you are when you're in action."

"First off, I do like the word 'charmed' quite a bit better; it's not nearly as crass as 'seduced.' And second of all, I do no such thing. I merely treat women, all women, with respect, and I listen to what they have to say, with all my attention. That's the only 'charm' I've ever had."

I thought about it, and suddenly I realized that most of what my grandfather had just told me was the complete and unvarnished truth. I'd never realized the source of his charm before. Evidently, a man of any age listening with *all* of his attention and not just some fraction of it was more enticing to most women than movie-star looks or a billionaire's money.

I was about to comment on it when the door we'd been watching suddenly opened. Instead of Helen Parsons, though, we were instantly faced with a large and angry man who looked perfectly capable of throwing us out of his office without anyone else's help, and more than ready to do just that. His hair was disheveled, and there was a fire in his eyes that was a little frightening. This was obviously a man it wouldn't do to get angry, but clearly we'd managed to do just that.

"What's this nonsense about me being tied to Roy Thompson's murder?" the mayor asked as he stared hard from Moose to me, and then back again.

"Do you really want to have this conversation out here where anyone can hear what we are discussing?" Moose asked him.

"I have nothing to hide," the mayor said angrily.

"Listen," Moose said, keeping his own voice calm and level. "I wasn't going to even bring this up if I didn't have to, but a friend of mine thinks it might be a good idea for you to talk to us."

"I'm not impressed by your friend, whoever he is," the mayor said, but I did notice that his tone of voice softened as soon as Moose made the statement.

"Judge Dixon will be saddened to learn that," Moose said, and then he turned to me and touched my arm lightly. "Let's go, Victoria. It's clear that we're wasting our time here."

I knew that he was bluffing, and I was pretty sure that the mayor probably realized it as well, but that didn't stop us from walking toward the outer door.

We never made it, though.

"Why don't you both come in and we can talk about it?" the mayor said.

I knew that grinning would be inappropriate, but it was still hard not to do it as Moose and I walked in. As we did, Ms. Parsons passed us, but there was no eye contact made between any of us. Evidently, we'd dropped all pretense of being friendly now.

The mayor's inner office was huge, expansive and a little too well-decorated for a town the size of Molly's Corners.

There was no way the town's budget could afford what I saw, from leather chairs to a massive mahogany desk that looked like a piece that belonged in a museum. Mayor Mullins took his place behind it as though it was the most natural place in the world for him to be, and as he did so, he gestured toward two close chairs. "Please, have a seat."

We did as we were told, but Moose didn't say a word after we sat, and neither did I.

After thirty seconds of silence, the mayor finally spoke. As he did, his voice was much calmer and more reasonable; it was about what I would expect from a civil servant. "Forgive my outburst earlier. It's been a trying day, and your misconception about Roy Thompson caught me completely off-guard."

"Then are you saying that you *didn't* have a business deal with Roy Thompson, one where you lost a substantial amount of money?" Moose asked gently.

"What might sound like a great deal of money to you is merely pocket change to me," the mayor said with the wave of a hand. "Look around. This office was furnished with my personal funds, not the town's coffers. If and when I'm voted out of office, it all goes with me."

"My, you must be rich," I said, speaking for the first time. "Surely you don't make that much from your day job."

The mayor looked at me fleetingly as he explained, "It's all old family money. I work because I want to, not because I need to. The business I had with Roy had an unfortunate outcome, but it was no one's fault, and certainly no reason to commit murder."

"I understand perfectly," Moose said with a smile that lacked much warmth at all. "If you'll tell us where you were earlier today from eleven to one, we'll be on our way and not bother you anymore."

"You must realize that I'm under no obligation to tell you that," he said, the ire rising a little in his voice as he spoke. Was there a bit of a hunted look in his eyes for one brief second? I couldn't be sure I'd actually seen it, it had flashed past so quickly.

"No, that's perfectly true," my grandfather told him. "I'm sure that Sheriff Croft will ask you himself after we've spoken. Let me remind you that since he's the county sheriff, you're under his jurisdiction as well."

The mayor clearly didn't like being outgunned, first with the judge, and then with the sheriff. "I have nothing to hide, but that doesn't mean that I'm going to share my whereabouts with you." He kept staring at his telephone as though willing it to ring, and seven seconds later, it did just that. The mayor nearly leapt out of his chair to answer it, and I suspected that it had been staged just for our benefit. "Yes, yes, I understand," he said gravely, and then hung up. "I'm sorry, but I'm needed elsewhere. Have a good day," he said as he stood.

Moose and I followed suit, and soon enough, the three of us walked out of his office together. The cop on duty looked surprised to see us being so chummy with the mayor, but he masked it well. "I'm truly sorry I don't have more time for you," Mayor Mullins said.

"We'd be glad to hang around until your emergency is over," I said with a polite smile, knowing that he'd never take us up on our offer.

"Thanks for your kindness, but this could take some time." He turned to the steps and headed for the second floor of the building, and for just a second, I thought about following him to see exactly what his 'emergency' was, but it wouldn't do us any good, and I knew it.

"Well, that was one colossal waste of time," I told Moose as we walked outside and got into his truck.

"What are you talking about? Were you in the same room as I was just now?"

"I don't follow," I told my grandfather.

"He's clearly hiding something," Moose said. "You could practically smell his fear in there."

"His pupils did dilate there for a second when you mentioned his alibi," I admitted. "Did we mess up just now,

Moose? What if we just gave the mayor a chance to put
something together before the sheriff could question him?"
It was one of my basic fears related to our investigations that
we would end up inadvertently helping the bad guys instead
of the good ones, and I hoped that wasn't what we'd just
done.

"Trust me, the man didn't act at all surprised by the news
of Roy's demise. He didn't even try to dispute the fact that
Roy had been murdered. When he came out of his office to
greet us the first time, it was pretty clear that he already knew
what had happened in Jasper Fork today. I'm willing to
wager that he's still working on something that will cover his
tail, and it has nothing to do with our visit. It will be for the
sheriff to determine, though. We've stirred the pot a little
more, and that's a good thing, as far as I'm concerned. Is
there anything else we can do in Molly's Corners, or should
we head back to the diner?"

"I vote we go to the diner," I said as I looked at my
watch. "If we hurry, I can relieve Martha before Jenny
shows up for her shift."

"Your grandmother doesn't mind working at The
Charming Moose; you know that, don't you?"

"I know, but I still don't like to take advantage of her
good nature any more than I have to."

"You're a good granddaughter, Victoria, just in case I
don't tell you enough."

I hugged him as I said, "As a matter of fact, you tell me
just enough."

"Could we keep my arrangements with the judge from
your grandmother?" he asked. "I still maintain that I did
nothing wrong, but there's no use causing trouble when there
isn't any reason to."

"I'll do one thing for you," I said. "I won't volunteer the
information, but if she asks, I'm telling her the truth."

"I can live with that," he said. The next bit was said
softly, and I doubted that it had been for my ears, but I heard
it nonetheless. "Let's just hope it doesn't come up."

GREG'S HOMEMADE CHICKEN NOODLE SOUP

This soup is a family favorite when one of us is sick, but we don't wait until then to have it as a wonderful lunch. It's based on my mother-in-law's family recipe, but of course, I've made it my own over the years, modifying it as the mood strikes me. This is especially delicious when it's served with grilled cheese sandwiches.
As an aside, my family likes their grilled cheese sandwiches these days made with mozzarella cheese, but cheddar is a wonderful choice as well. I've found that the key to a great grilled cheese sandwich is to grill it slowly, with butter on both sides of the bread, to give the cheese plenty of time to melt into gooey goodness.

Ingredients

1 Tablespoon butter, unsalted
2-3 carrots, medium, peeled and chopped
1 onion, medium sized, diced.

1-2 cans chicken broth, 99% fat free (14.5 to 29 oz)
1-2 cups chicken, cooked and cut into bite-sized chunks
1 teaspoon basil, dried
2 dashes salt, regular table variety
2 dashes pepper, regular table variety

1 to 1/1/2 cups noodles, cooked (we like wide egg noodles in our soup)
Enough water to boil the noodles

Directions

In a large pan, melt the butter over low heat, and then add the carrots and onion, cooking them until they soften slightly.

Next, add the chicken broth (the amount depends on the consistency you like. We prefer a less soupy mix and more of a stew texture, so we just use one can), basil, salt and pepper. Bring this to a boil, and then simmer for 10 to 15 minutes on low heat.

In another pot, cook the noodles until they are done per the directions on the package. After they're finished cooking, drain them, and then add the noodles to the simmering broth mixture.

Next up, add the cut up chicken pieces, stir them in together well, and then heat the entire soup throughout over low to low-medium heat. Serve this soup with grilled cheese sandwiches, and you've got a wonderful meal!

Chapter 6

"Welcome back, you two," Martha said as Moose and I walked back into the diner half an hour later. "I didn't expect you both back so soon."

"Neither did we, but our last appointment had a sudden emergency he had to take care of," I explained with a smile.

"Yes, I believe he was called away for something quite dire," Moose kicked in. "Evidently, it was all just one big coincidence that it happened exactly after we asked him for his alibi. It's funny how things work out sometimes."

"Do you think he was the one responsible for what happened to Roy Thompson?" Martha asked him gravely.

"It's way too soon to tell, one way or the other. After all, the man was just poisoned today."

I looked around the diner and was troubled to see that we had only one customer at the time, and it was a woman I didn't recognize. Had all of our regulars deserted us already? Word might not have had a chance to get out earlier, but if this was the result of that happening, what did that spell for The Charming Moose? "Has it been this slow since we've been gone?"

Martha shrugged. "It has, but Victoria, you know as well as I do that from two to four, there's never a big crowd in here."

"I know that it's true in my mind, but in my heart, there's an entirely different reason for it today. I hope we solve this one quickly."

"I'm sure you will," Martha said, trying her best to be reassuring. "So, are you both back for good, or do I need to stay here longer?"

"I've got a hunch that we're done for the day," I said, remembering the sheriff's caveat that we weren't to approach his three main witnesses until the next day at noon. "What do you think, Moose? Do you have any more ideas we can pursue?"

"Not at the moment, but we both know that could all change with one telephone call. There are a few feelers I put out that are still working on answers."

I grabbed the order pad from my grandmother. "Well, until something else happens, why don't you two take off? I'm sure you have better things to do than just hang around the diner all night."

"Are you kicking us out, Granddaughter?" Moose asked me deadpan.

"Let's just say I'm saving you for when I really need you both, and leave it at that," I replied. "Shall we?"

"When you two are finished teasing each other, I'd like to go home, Moose."

"I don't see any reason why not. We've done all that we can for now," Moose said. "What did you have in mind?" he asked as he winked broadly at Martha.

"You'll just have to wait until we get there to find out," she said as she smiled at her husband.

"I'll call you later if something comes up," Moose told me on his way out the door.

"I'm counting on it," I said.

After they were gone, I refilled the lone diner's coffee cup, and then I asked her, "Can I get you anything else?"

The woman frowned a little, looked around at the empty diner, and then she said, "You're Victoria, aren't you?"

"I am," I said as I offered my hand. "And who might you be?"

"Someone who wants to talk to you in private," she said. I couldn't get over how helpless she looked, as though she needed someone bigger and stronger to take care of her. "My name is Loretta Jenkins. I'm Roy Thompson's illegitimate daughter."

"You sure know how to start a conversation," I told her as I sat down across from her. "I'm sorry, but I didn't even realize that Roy had any children besides Asher."

"He didn't have any that he ever claimed, that's for sure," she said with a hint of sadness in her voice. Loretta was a pretty woman in her early thirties, and knowing Roy, her mother must have been a real beauty for her to come out looking that good from that particular gene pool mix. Loretta had striking brown eyes, and hair so black that it almost didn't look natural. She was petite, barely over five feet tall, and if she weighed a hundred pounds soaking wet, I'd eat my raincoat.

"Might I ask who your mother is?"

"You may. And it's was now. Momma's name was Honey Jenkins. She met Roy when he was sizing up some property he was thinking about buying, and from the way she told it, their attraction was nothing more than two lonely people getting together for one night. When she got pregnant, she contacted him, but he never got back to her. I didn't find that last part out about until last month after Momma passed away. I was going through her things, and I found a rough draft of one of her letters to him. It was all pretty sad, and I was wondering how to handle it when I found out that Roy had been murdered."

"Loretta, how did you get the news that quickly?" I asked her. "This all just happened this afternoon."

"Oddly enough, I was in town trying to decide if I was ready to tell him about me when I heard that he died. I guess I'll never get the chance to get to know him now."

If it were true, it was one of the saddest stories I'd ever heard in my life.

"I'm sorry for your loss, but why tell me?" I asked her.

"I heard around town that you were digging into his murder, and I didn't want to talk to the police about my connection with Roy if I didn't have to."

"Why not? That would seem like the next logical step for you to take," I asked.

"Well," she said, suddenly not making eye contact with me anymore. "I have a few issues with the police. Nothing serious, just some outstanding parking tickets and things like that. I was kind of hoping to avoid all that by talking to you. Have you figured out who killed him yet?"

"My grandfather and I are good, but it just happened less than five hours ago," I said. "These things take time, and we've just gotten started. I'd ask you if you knew anyone with a motive to kill your father, but from the sound of it, you didn't really even know the man."

"That's true, but honestly, *I* might have a motive. I wasn't going to push it before, but now that he's gone, I'm going to make sure that I get my share of what's coming to me." I must have looked surprised by her callous admission, because she quickly followed that up with, "I never had a father, just a series of my mom's boyfriends. Roy Thompson can't leave a legacy behind in my heart, but he sure can make up for it in my wallet."

Wow, and she'd struck me as such a quiet, almost helpless woman at first glance. How quickly that had changed once she opened her mouth and started talking.

"Well, I have nothing to do with his estate, and so far, I have no idea who might have killed him."

She nodded, slid a five under her plate, and then stood. "If you come up with anything, I live in Laurel Landing with my boyfriend." She jotted down her number on a torn-off edge of her placemat, and handed it to me. "I'd appreciate it if you'd let me know what's going on."

"You really do need to talk to the sheriff," I said. "He's not going to care about some parking tickets. He'll want to interview you as soon as possible."

"I'm sorry, but that's something he just can't do," she said firmly, and I could see an edge coming out of her that reminded me of her late father. There was steel there buried beneath the surface, an unexpected strength of will. "I trust that you'll keep my little secret all to yourself. Otherwise, I wouldn't take kindly to it."

"I'm not making you any promises," I said, startled by her veiled threat.

"You might want to reconsider that," Loretta said as she stood.

After she left the diner, I walked back to the kitchen. Greg was already standing in the doorway.

"Did you hear any of that?" I asked him.

"Just the part where she threatened you," Greg said. "That woman is trouble."

"I've got a hunch that you're right. What should I do?"

To his credit, my husband didn't even hesitate. "Call Sheriff Croft, tell him what just happened, and give him that telephone number."

"You're not worried that she might try to retaliate?"

"You can't let that influence you," Greg said. "The sheriff has a right to know, and besides, you've got a whole clan watching your back. *Nobody* threatens one of our own and gets away with it."

I kissed my husband lightly, and then I pulled out my cell phone.

The sheriff answered on the first ring, and I said, "Sheriff Croft, we have to talk."

"Is it about Roy Thompson's murder?" he asked, "because otherwise, I'm not interested."

"Let me ask you something. Did you know that Roy had an illegitimate daughter named Loretta Jenkins?"

There was a moment's pause on the other end as he processed the information, and then the sheriff asked, "Do I even want to know how you came by that particular bit of information?"

"I didn't do a thing," I explained. "Apparently she came to the diner looking for me, and after she asked me for some information I didn't have, she gave me a pretty clear threat not to tell you."

"Is she still there?"

"No, after she threatened me, she walked out the door."

"It's a shame she didn't hang around," the sheriff said. "Do you have any idea where she lives?"

"She said that she's in Laurel Landing, but I can do better

than that. I've got her telephone number, if that might help."

"Let's have it," he said, and I read the number off the piece of paper she'd given me. "Victoria, you did the right thing calling me."

"There was never any doubt in my mind," I said as I winked at my husband.

"Would you like me to send someone over there?" the sheriff asked.

"She doesn't even know that I've told you yet," I said. "Besides, we can take care of ourselves here."

"I'm sure you believe that, but I'm still going to ask some of my patrol officers to double up patrolling the diner and your house for a while."

"Do you honestly think she knows where I live?" I asked, suddenly a little unnerved that Loretta Jenkins might have that knowledge. The diner was one thing, but my home was my sanctuary, a place that Greg and I shared away from The Charming Moose.

"With the technology available these days, I wouldn't doubt it for a second," he said. "I'm going to make her my top priority."

"Then you should know that she already admitted to me that she was in town today when her dad was poisoned."

"Slow down a second. We don't even know for sure that Roy was her biological father," the sheriff said.

"You won't think that after you've spoken with her. She acts like a chip off the old block, and I don't mean that in a good way."

"Understood," the sheriff said. "Thanks for the tip, Victoria."

"You're welcome." I was about to ask him if he'd made any real progress on the case, but he hung up before I had the chance. Maybe he'd done that on purpose, just to stall my inevitable questions that were sure to follow.

After I hung up my phone and started to put it away, Greg asked, "Aren't you going to call Moose and tell him what just happened?"

"I suppose I'd better, but he's not going to be too pleased with me."

"Why not?" Greg asked. "You did everything you could."

"You and I both know that, but I'm sure that in Moose's mind, he's going to be disappointed that I didn't lock Loretta in the bathroom until he could get here so he could grill her himself."

Greg smiled at that reference. "You still need to call him."

I did as my husband suggested, and as predicted, Moose was unhappy that I hadn't been able to get more out of Loretta, but mostly he took it in stride.

"At the very least, we have another motivated suspect to add to our list," Moose said. "If she was telling you the truth, greed might be a factor in her committing murder."

"But why now?" I asked. "Wouldn't she want to take the opportunity to meet the man who was her father before she killed him?"

"He might have been the biological contributor, but from the sound of things, he did nothing to help raise her, emotionally or financially. From the sound of this woman, she must be pretty cold."

"Icy," I agreed.

"Don't worry about a thing, Victoria. You did the right thing calling the sheriff."

"Even despite her warning not to say anything?" I asked.

"Our family never lets threats keep us from doing what we think is right," Moose said. "We never have, and we're not about to start now."

"No matter what might happen because of this?" I asked. For some reason, this petite woman's threat had unnerved me more than if it had been uttered by a two-hundred pound madman.

"No matter what," Moose replied.

The rest of the evening was fairly quiet, and though we

weren't anywhere near our usual number of diners throughout the remainder of our time open, the drop-off wasn't so large that a casual observer would notice it.

I knew, though.

We wouldn't feel the losses much at the cash register, but if this trend continued, The Charming Moose could be in some serious trouble.

"Are you ready to head home?" Greg asked me as he came up front from the kitchen area. "Everything's set back in the back."

"Almost; I need one more second," I said. Since Martha had spent some time working the cash register, I was running into a few discrepancies, nothing too large to worry about too much, but enough to make me scratch my head and wonder how she'd managed to come up with four dollars and twenty seven cents more than the report showed we should have. I balanced out the tape with the irregular entry, and then I did my best not to think about it.

After zipping the money, credit card receipts, and our deposit slip into a bank bag, I turned to Greg and said, "I'm as ready as I'll ever be."

"How bad was it?" he asked with a grin as he pointed to the night-deposit bag.

"All I can say is that it could have been worse," I replied.

"In the end, that's the best we can hope for, isn't it?"

"I suppose so," I said. "I just wish that it wasn't necessary for Martha to pitch in so much around here. She's earned her retirement, and she should be able to enjoy it."

"You don't see her when she's working," Greg said. "I wouldn't worry about your grandmother at all. She might not be great with the register, but folks absolutely love her, and it's clear that the feeling is mutual."

I nodded absently, and Greg pressed me a bit. "Victoria, you seem down. Is there anything I can do to help?"

"Not unless you know the identity of who killed Roy Thompson," I said.

Greg shrugged a little. "Sorry, but that's one area where I can't help you out."

I nodded. "I know. Don't get me wrong; it would have been bad enough if Roy had been killed with something else today, but the fact that it was your dessert makes it a thousand times worse. Greg, why aren't you more upset about it than you seem to be? After all, you're the one who made that cake."

"I don't deny it, but whoever put poison in that slice killed Roy, not me. I can't change what happened. You and Moose are trying to find out who did it, so what's left for me to do? Worrying won't solve a thing, so I refuse to let it steal a single minute of my life that it doesn't have to."

"I just wish that I felt the way you do," I admitted. "Sometimes I really envy your happy disposition."

He took me in his arms and hugged me. "Well, we're even. I admire your willingness to put yourself in harm's way just to be sure that justice is done. You don't give yourself enough credit for the things you do, and more important than that, the things you *are*."

"How did I get so lucky finding you?" I asked as I stared into my husband's eyes.

"I like to think that we're *both* lucky," Greg said.

I was about to reply when I saw the hint of a frown forming on his lips. "What's wrong? Did you change your mind about being lucky that fast?"

"No, it's not that. To be honest with you, I planned a surprise for you for tonight, but I'm not sure it's the best time to spring it on you now."

That was so sweet of him. "If it's a happy surprise, it's always welcome," I said. "You should know that by now."

"That's good, because I can't wait."

I hesitated a few seconds, and then I asked him, "What are you waiting for? Let's have it," I said as I stuck my hands out greedily.

"I don't have it *on* me," Greg said with a laugh. "You'll have to wait until we get home to get it."

"Exactly what kind of surprise are we talking about here, Greg?"

He laughed as I raised one eyebrow. "Victoria, I can give you two hints. It stays outside all of the time, and I had to have help to make it happen."

I bit my lower lip as I considered the possibilities. "Those have to be two of the worst hints ever in the history of the Guessing Game."

"That's because you're not supposed to guess. I'm afraid that you're just going to have to wait until we get home."

"Then, what are we standing around here for?" I asked him. "Let's go."

"Yes, Ma'am, but we're still stopping by the bank first."

"You're no fun at all," I said with a laugh as we turned off the last few lights. Once that was accomplished, we locked the diner up for the night, got into our separate cars, and then Greg and I drove home together in single file. Since we worked such divergent shifts during the course of the day, it was a rare closing that found us both in the same vehicle at the end of the working day.

When we got home, I parked first as I looked wildly around the front yard, but I couldn't see anything out of the ordinary. "I thought you said that it was outside," I said as I met Greg when he opened his door.

"Have a little patience. It's supposed to be in back," he said as he took my hand and led me through the side yard. It was growing chilly out, and I instinctively walked a little closer to my husband, as though I was trying to draw some warmth from his presence. I didn't care what was waiting for me in the back, no matter how sweet the gesture was. I promised myself that I'd spend at least thirty seconds admiring it after the unveiling, but then I was going to head straight inside, make some hot cocoa, and settle in for the night. It had been a long and trying day, and I for one was ready to see the end of it.

However, my husband clearly had other plans.

Chapter 7

"What is it?" I asked my husband as we stumbled around in the dark. "Can't we have some kind of light back here?"

"We could, but I don't want to spoil the surprise," Greg said.

"If I'm in the hospital because I tripped and fell, there won't be any surprise at all. I can always close my eyes, if that would help."

I heard him laugh. "Victoria, if you close your eyes, how will that be any different from the way things are right now?"

"Well, at least, then, *one* of us will be able to see," I said with a smile.

"Too late. We're already here." Greg flipped the switch to our outdoor lights in back, and I saw the new addition instantly.

"It's the gas fire-pit I've had my eye on for months," I said as I raced to it. "How did you manage to do this?"

"Jack Kiley at the hardware store owed me a favor, so he came over and set this up on his lunch break. There should already be propane in it," he said as he knelt down to check. "I told him to leave some spare one-pound tanks. Look at that. They fit in your hand. Here are some matches, too," Greg said happily. "Jack's really on the ball. So, should I go ahead and light it?"

"I can't wait," I said as I pulled two chairs over to where the new pit was stationed. The propane went up with a satisfying whoosh, and in an instant, we had fire. "Wow, that's a lot faster than getting a fire started in our old pit." I looked over six yards to our original wood burning fire pit. Greg and I had enjoyed a lot of roasted marshmallows around that pit in the past. "We don't have to get rid of Old Smokey just because we have this one now, do we?"

"No, Jack told me that this one doesn't put out a lot of

heat. It's more here for the dancing flames, and the fact that we can have a ten minute fire whenever we want one. If we want some real heat, we'll still have to fire up the wood-burning pit."

"I feel so *rich* having both of them," I said with a laugh. "Are you sure we can afford such decadence?"

"I think we've earned it," he said. "Besides, it wasn't *that* much. So, what do you say? Would you like to hang out around here a little, or should we shut it off and go inside?"

I shivered a little and warmed my hands near the fire. While it was true that the heat it put off couldn't touch its wood-burning brother, it still managed to toast them nicely. "I can stay out a little if you can."

"Tell you what," Greg said. "Why don't we wait until it warms up a little? I just wanted you to have this now whenever you wanted a little fire."

"It's wonderful," I said, and then I kissed my husband soundly.

"Do you really like it?"

"How could I not love it? After all, *you* got it for me."

Greg laughed. "Don't forget, I got you those red and green socks one year for Christmas, too, and you haven't worn them since."

I smiled back at him, happy yet again that he was all mine. "That's because I'm saving them for a special occasion. It wouldn't do to wear them out."

"No, by all means, save them," he replied. I loved to hear the happiness in his voice. He'd surprised me—something I admitted was not that easy to do—with something I'd truly wanted. I knew all about that particular sense of elation, because it was the same feeling I got when I managed to reverse roles and do it for him.

As Greg leaned over to turn off the propane feed to the flames, I said, "Leave it on for another few minutes. I love watching the flames dance in the wind."

"That's something we can't do with our old fire-pit,"

Greg said. "It would be too dangerous."

"Shh, not so loud; she might hear you," I said.

Greg didn't comment, other than to shake his head and smile.

Things were good, at least they were at home between us. It was a shame that murder had to intrude on our lives. Without that, I just might be able to say that my life was perfect exactly the way it was. Sure, we could have used more money, and even more important, more time together, but what we had was pretty excellent, and I wasn't about to take one second of it for granted.

"Mom, what happened here?" I asked my mother in dismay the next morning as I neared the diner. It was still dark out, but there was enough light coming from the street so I could see the glass window at the front of the diner. Someone had painted a giant X through the lettering in bright red paint, Mom had brought out a bucket and rag with her from inside.

"My guess is that vandals were having a little fun at our expense," she said as she started to wipe the wet rag through the paint.

"That's not going to work," I said just as the paint started to smear. How odd. "That shouldn't happen, should it?"

"It's not real paint," Mom said as she dunked her rag back into the bucket, and then she cleaned away the smeared edge she'd just made.

"It looks real enough to me," I said.

"Somebody must have bought some of that special paint folks use to decorate their windows for Christmas. It washes off easily enough. I suppose it could have been a lot worse. I swear, sometimes I wonder what teenagers do with themselves these days."

"What makes you think that teenagers did it?" I asked as I took the rag from her and reached a few areas she couldn't get to. She was right about one thing; the paint came off easily enough when it got wet.

"Well, if they'd meant any real harm, they wouldn't have bothered with the paint, now would they? If someone wanted to send us a message, a rock through the window would have been quite a bit more effective, don't you think?"

I didn't even want to consider the possibility of how bad a mess broken glass would have made, but I still couldn't accept the fact that this was just a random act of mischief.

We had just about finished cleaning the window when a squad car drove up, and the driver parked in such a way that his headlights reflected off our glass.

Sheriff Croft got out, and then he nodded in our direction. "Melinda, Victoria. It's awfully early to be Spring cleaning, isn't it?"

"Someone spray-painted a big red X on our window," I told him.

"So, they got you, too?"

"What do you mean, too? Who else got tagged with paint?"

The sheriff pointed toward the square. "I've seen four other businesses so far myself, and I just got started." He studied our window, and then he asked, "How'd you get it so clean? Is that just soap and water in your bucket?"

Mom explained, "It's just temporary paint, Sheriff. I keep telling Victoria that it's random mischief, but she doesn't believe me."

The sheriff turned to me. "You haven't been interviewing my suspects behind my back, have you?"

"We haven't talked to *anyone* on your list," I said, happy that I could tell him the absolute truth.

"That means that you've started a list of your own, then, doesn't it?" he asked.

"How could you possibly know that?" Mom asked.

"It just figures, Melinda. If your daughter truly believes that someone is warning her off of her investigation, that means that she had to have spoken to at least one person she believes is a suspect, and most likely it's more than one."

"Why do you say that?" I asked. He was right, but I

wasn't about to give him the satisfaction of acknowledging anything he said at the moment.

"If there was just one suspect, you'd have mentioned them by name. Now, why don't we all go inside, have some coffee, and you can tell me all about it? There *is* coffee, isn't there?"

"I just brewed a fresh batch," Mom said with a smile. "Come on in, and I'll pour you some."

Sheriff Croft rubbed his hands together to ward off the chill, and then he smiled. "I don't mind if I do."

We went inside, and Mom started flipping on all of the overhead lights. I wondered when she'd had time to make coffee, but then I realized that she'd had to come back outside once she got the soap, water, and the rag, so she must have flipped the coffee pot on as she'd walked past it. I grabbed three cups, but Mom shook her head. "None for me. I get jumpy when I start drinking caffeine this early. I'm going to go into the kitchen and get things started. Cleaning off all of that paint put me a little behind."

"That's fine," I said, and then I returned one of the cups to the stack. I grabbed the pot, topped off two cups, and then delivered them to the counter where the sheriff was sitting.

He took a sip, and then smiled. "That's awfully good."

"Have you been up all night?" I asked.

"Do I look that rough?" he responded. "I got up an hour ago, but it's true that I was up late last night. The work of a county sheriff never seems to get finished, and the lines between days and nights sometimes blur together more than I'd like."

I decided to cut the man a little slack. I had an inkling of how hard he worked, but I was certain that, overall, I didn't have any idea what the entire scope of his responsibilities were.

"So, who have you and your grandfather been speaking to about Roy Thompson?" he asked after another sip.

"Well, we did have a little luck," I admitted. "But first, tell me what happened when you spoke with Loretta Jenkins.

Do you think she's telling the truth about Roy being her father?"

"As a matter of fact, I couldn't find her, though it wasn't from lack of trying. She wasn't at her apartment, and I didn't have any luck tracking that cell phone number down, either. Are you sure that she gave you the right number?"

"I'm positive," I said. "Honest, I didn't just make her up. Greg and Martha saw her, too."

"I'm not doubting that someone came in here claiming to be Roy's daughter, but I can't do anything about her until I actually see the woman myself. If she comes back here today, give me a call, would you?"

"Of course," I said. That was odd. Where was Loretta all of a sudden?

"So, who's the next name on your list?" he asked after he took another sip.

"We're also looking at the mayor from Molly's Corners," I said.

The sheriff looked startled to hear that name. "Hank Mullins? Why in the world would he kill Roy Thompson?"

"They had a business deal that went bad," I said.

"And you know that how, exactly?" he asked, and then he quickly changed his mind. "Forget I asked. I'm not at all sure that I want to know. How much would it take for Hank to kill him? From what I've heard, the man's richer than most."

"He claimed that it was pocket change for him, but we don't believe him."

The sheriff shrugged. "I'll look into it. Thanks for the tip."

"Do you have *anything* that you can share with me?" I asked. "After all, I just spilled my guts to you."

He shook his head. "Sorry, but I'm really not ready to share yet."

"Maybe not, but our deal still stands, Sheriff. Come noon, Moose and I are free of our promise."

"I wanted to talk to you about that," Sheriff Croft said

hesitantly, and I didn't like the tone of his voice.

"Hang on one second. Don't try to renege. We had a deal."

"I know that, and I'm not going back on my word. I just wish the two of you would give me more time before you tackle those four. I've got a hunch that one of them is about to crack."

"That's easy, then," I said.

"I don't like how quickly you agreed to my request," the sheriff said, and then he took another sip of his coffee.

"I didn't agree to anything," I countered. "Just tell me who you think is going to confess, and we'll go after the other three the second it hits twelve o'clock noon."

"That's not going to happen, Victoria," Sheriff Croft said with a frown just as Mom came back out front.

He stood, laid a dollar by his cup, and said, "That's some mighty fine coffee, Melinda. Thank you kindly."

"That's why we're here," she said with a smile, and the sheriff left.

"What was that all about?" my mother asked me.

"I don't know what you're talking about."

"Young lady, I know that expression. What did he just say to you?"

I finally admitted, "The sheriff came by to ask us for too big a favor, and I had to turn him down."

"That explains the frown," Mom said. "Are you sure you didn't have any choice?"

"No," I said flatly. "He prides himself on his word being his bond just as much as we do, and he's not about to break it. Maybe next time he won't be so quick to promise something that he might regret later, but for right now, our deal stands."

"I'm not happy when you and your grandfather are at odds with the police," Mom said as she took the sheriff's cup and put it in a plastic tub behind the counter.

"I'm not all that fond of it myself, but I really didn't have much choice. Every hour that Roy Thompson's murder goes unsolved is another hour folks might think that we were responsible for it. We can't stay in business if we don't have any customers, and if people around here begin to believe that we poisoned that cake ourselves, there won't be a diner much longer."

"I know you're doing what you have to for The Charming Moose," Mom said as she lightly touched my arm. "Did I hear someone mention something happening at noon?"

"You did," I said. "Moose is asking Martha to cover for me then so we can continue our investigation, but I'll be here this morning for my regular shift."

The front door opened, and our early morning waitress, Ellen Hightower, came in, looking more disheveled than normal. "Sorry I'm late, but my car wouldn't start. I'm afraid that it's on its last legs."

"Is it really that serious?" I asked her. We depended on Ellen to see us through our breakfast and lunch times, and if she couldn't get to the diner, she wouldn't do us much good.

"Don't worry; Wayne at the car repair place is going to look at it for me today. I think he's kind of sweet on me, so he promised me that the bill wouldn't be too bad."

"I didn't know the two of you were going out," I said.

"We're not, but that doesn't keep him from asking."

"You really should go out with him," Mom said as she smiled. My mother believed that everyone should have someone in their lives, and she wasn't shy about sharing her opinion. "He's really cute."

Ellen blushed a little. "I know, but with my kids, it's tough to make time to actually have a personal life of my own."

"If you wait until they're all gone, you'll miss out on too many opportunities," Mom said. "Tell you what. Go ahead and make a date with the man, and I'll provide the babysitting services, free of charge."

"I couldn't ask you to do that," Ellen said.

"You didn't ask. I volunteered, remember? Come on. What do you have to lose? Like the man said, you don't have anything to fear but fear itself."

"FDR wasn't talking about dating when he said that," I reminded my mother. Somebody had to rein her in.

"Well, it applies to this just the same." She turned to Ellen and asked, "When's the last time you went out on a real date?"

"There hasn't been anyone since Luke left me," she said. "I wouldn't even know how to go about it. What am I supposed to do, ask *him* out?"

"You could do it if you wanted to, but I have a hunch that if you just smile at him, he'll ask you again."

"I don't know," Ellen said, but I could see the hint of a smile as she ducked her head down.

"Just don't close any doors. That's all I ask," Mom said as the diner's front door opened and a handful of construction men came in, laughing and teasing each other about something.

As Ellen greeted them and followed them to their table, I told my mother, "You never give up, do you?"

"What? Can't a gal do a friend a favor? Ellen deserves some happiness in her life."

"How can you be so sure that Wayne can deliver it?" I asked her.

"Come on. He's a sweetheart, and you know it. They belong together; they just don't realize it yet."

"You are a romantic through and through, aren't you?" I asked.

"I don't deny it, and what's more, I wouldn't have it any other way," she said. "If I hadn't gone after your father, you wouldn't be here today, so I wouldn't knock my romantic tendencies if I were you, Victoria."

"Funny, I always thought that Dad was the one who pursued you," I said.

"He thinks so, too, so let's keep this just between us."

Ellen approached with the orders, and Mom took them from her with a smile. As she walked back into the kitchen, she started humming, and it took me a second to figure out what the song was. Then I finally got it. *Love Is in the Air.* I wasn't sure how appropriate it was, but I had to give my mother credit. When it came to romance, she never gave up.

The rest of my first shift was relatively uneventful, and I for one was happy about it. The investigation was just getting fully underway, but I was already beginning to resent the time it was taking away from my shifts at the diner. I had the wackiest schedule imaginable, on from six to eight, eleven to four, and five to seven, but it suited me, and it disrupted my entire life when it didn't work out that way.

I got home after my first shift in plenty of time to make my husband some breakfast, and we even managed to enjoy a little hot chocolate afterwards in our backyard enjoying our new propane fire-pit before we both had to go in to work. It was with some reluctance that we went to the diner just before eleven, and if I'd known what Moose was planning to do, I might have skipped my middle shift entirely.

Unfortunately, though, I didn't have the gift of foresight, so when Greg and I walked into the diner a little before eleven, my grandfather jumped on me before I even had the chance to take off my coat.

Chapter 8

"It's about time you two showed up," Moose said as he ambushed me from behind the register. Greg looked bemused by it all, but he didn't say a word.

"I'm not due in for another two minutes," I said as I took my coat off. "Besides, we promised the sheriff that we wouldn't start our investigation until noon, so we've got another hour. What's the rush, anyway? Martha's not even here yet."

"She's in the kitchen chatting with your mother," Moose said. "I heard about the little bit of excitement you had around here earlier."

"Has she been telling you about Ellen and Wayne?" I asked.

"No. What are you talking about, girl?"

"Mom is playing matchmaker again," I said.

"I'm talking about someone marking up our diner," Moose said. "There aren't many ways to read a bloody X on the window, are there?"

"So, you don't think that it's random, either?" I asked, relieved that at least one person agreed with me.

"How could it be? We started investigating a murder, and the next thing you know, someone's targeting us."

"There's another explanation, you know," Greg said.

"I'd like to hear what it might be," Moose said. "And don't give me any nonsense about it being random teens, because I don't believe it."

"My cake killed Roy Thompson. Maybe someone marked the diner as a place where no one should take a chance eating."

I rubbed my husband's shoulder in support. "That's nonsense, Greg. Nobody blames you for what happened to Roy."

"It's hard to tell just *how* many folks around here believe it, Victoria."

"It's true, my boy," Moose said. "You were the wronged party here."

"Well, it didn't work out too well for Roy, either, did it?"

I was about to say something when my mother came out of the kitchen. She smiled at my husband the second she saw him. "There you are. The kitchen's all yours. I wasn't sure you were coming today, Greg."

"Have I ever let you down, Mom?" he asked, and she smiled broadly. It had taken her some time and persuasion to get him from Mrs. Nelson to Melinda, and even longer to modify that to Mom, but she'd finally managed to do it. The funny thing was that Dad was still Mr. Nelson to him, and I doubted that there was anything that would ever change that. I didn't know how my father felt about it, but if he minded the formal honorific, he never said anything about it, at least not in my presence.

"And I know that you never will," she said as she patted his cheek gently. After greeting Greg, Mom turned to her father-in-law. "Moose, will you leave the poor girl alone? I heard her tell the sheriff this morning that you couldn't start digging until noon, and you shouldn't be tempting her to start early."

"Melinda," he said with a smile, "why don't you worry about romance and leave murder to me?"

She shook her head and laughed. "I see someone's been talking behind my back."

"And in front of it, as well," I said.

"Are you all talking about me?" Ellen asked as she cleaned a nearby table.

"Whatever gave you that idea?" I asked with a smile.

She just laughed it off, waved the rag in the air, and then she went back to cleaning.

"Since you're here now, I'm off," Mom said, and kissed my cheek as she went past me.

"None for me?" Moose asked her with that devilish grin

of his.

"I know I shouldn't encourage you, but I can't seem to help myself," she said as she kissed his cheek as well.

After my mother was gone, Moose turned to me. "So, what do you say? If we start interviewing folks now, we can get an hour's jump on things."

"I say no, and I shouldn't have to tell you the reason why," I said, scolding him a little with my tone of voice.

If it bothered him in the least, he didn't show it. "Fine, but I still think it's a bad idea to just sit around here and wait."

"Maybe so, but we gave our word," I said, and then I instantly regretted it.

Moose must have seen something in my face. "What's wrong, Victoria?"

"I have no idea how we're going to keep our promise now," I said as I pointed over his shoulder.

We weren't going after any of our suspects, but one of them was about to walk right into our diner, and I wasn't sure just how much we could talk about until noon came around.

"Kelly, I'm surprised to see you here. Have you ever even been to the diner?"

As she walked in, I could have sworn I saw Asher outside on the sidewalk, but when I looked back, whoever had been there was gone now. If it *had* been Asher, had he had the same idea to come in to talk to us about his father's murder? I hoped that he'd come back after Kelly was gone. I wanted to speak to both of them, and doing it at the diner was much preferred, since it was on our home turf.

Kelly shook her head. "Actually, I'm allergic to so many things, it's nearly impossible for me to find something to eat out anywhere I go. It's quite lovely," Roy Thompson's secretary/receptionist said as she looked around.

The Charming Moose could be called many things, but I wasn't sure that 'lovely' was one of them. Sure, we had our own eclectic charm, and the jukebox in the corner gave us a little color, but I knew what we had. It was a place to come when you wanted to feel as though you were home, surrounded by friendly people, heavenly aromas, and food that made you feel as though you'd never left your childhood home. Some folks called it a hole, some a dive, but I didn't mind. I knew better than most what it was, and I loved it because of that, not in spite of it.

"Thank you for your kind words," I said. "If you didn't come by for the food, what can we do for you?"

"Well, I *do* drink coffee," she said with a smile.

"Then pick a seat, and I'll fix you right up," I told her. "If you tell my husband the things that you *can* have, I'm sure he could come up with *something* for you to eat."

"Actually, I'm not really hungry. I was hoping to get a chance to speak with you and Moose about my boss, though."

I was on the horns of a dilemma now. Did this qualify as going after a suspect in the sheriff's mind? After all, she'd walked into our place of her own free will. I felt as though I had abided by the sheriff's demand that we not go after her, but I didn't want him stopping by before noon and seeing my grandfather and me grilling someone on his forbidden list.

I was still debating the ethical quandary when Moose settled it for the both of us. "There's nothing we'd like more. Follow me," he said as he led her to a table away from everyone else. I had no choice but to trail along behind them. I might not believe that we were in the clear one hundred percent with the sheriff, but that didn't mean that I was going to be left out of the conversation, either. Ethics was one thing, but this was something else entirely.

I grabbed three cups and the coffee pot, and after we were all settled in, Kelly said, "I suppose you think it's odd that I'm coming to you two, but you were so interested in Mr. Thompson's murder that I felt as though we all want the same thing, to figure out who killed him. The sheriff was so cold and official when we spoke that it seemed to me as though he was following some kind of script. To be honest with you, the man intimidates the daylights out of me."

I wasn't about to say anything bad about Sheriff Croft, and I needed to stop Moose from doing it, either. "He has boundaries and restrictions that we don't," I said. "Given his limitation, he's very good at what he does."

"Maybe so," Kelly said, "but there's a lot more to it than that. I've asked around, and I understand now why you two started your investigation. This isn't the first time you've looked for a killer, is it?"

"We've been thrown into a few situations in the past," my grandfather admitted rather humbly. We both knew full well that there was a lot more to it than that. We'd actively tracked murderers before when our motivations had been strong enough. Having a murder victim die after eating a piece of our cake gave us both more than reason enough to dig into what had happened.

"You solved them, though, didn't you?" she asked.

"We did, one way or another," I replied. "Is there anything you can add to what you told us yesterday?"

"Oh, there's lots more I know now," she said as she dug into her purse and started digging through it. After nearly a full minute, she pulled out the back of a Chinese take-out menu, and I saw that it was nearly covered with notes and names. Kelly appeared to be quite dynamic in her musings, because I saw a host of exclamation marks, bold stars, and heavy outlines marking up the paper.

"May I see that?" I asked, curious about the intensity of her note-taking.

She just laughed. "I'd give it to you, but I'm afraid that you wouldn't be able to make anything out of it. I tend to ramble when I do this, so without me as a guide, you couldn't make heads or tails of the whole thing. It's a lot easier if I just tell you what I found out."

"I understand," I said, though that wasn't quite true. "Go on, and we'll both try to follow along."

"Here goes," she said as she studied the back of the menu. It appeared that, at least at first, she was having trouble herself knowing exactly where to begin. After a few moments though, she nodded, and then the words began tumbling out of her mouth as though she had less than a minute to live. "James Manchester threatened Roy before, around the time someone ran Roy off the road in his car. Are they connected? I think they might be. Sylvia Jones tried to get Roy arrested for domestic violence when they were married, even though I'm positive that it never happened. A long time ago, his son, Asher, threatened him with a .22 caliber pistol when he was sixteen because Roy wouldn't buy him a Corvette. I found out that Hank Mullins was his mystery partner, and evidently the mayor lost more than he could handle in one of their deals. He's not nearly as rich as he pretends to be." She peered at the menu again, and then added, "I was looking through Roy's calendar, and I saw that he had an appointment that he never told me about last night. It was with someone with the initials L.J., but I've gone through all our files, and I can't find anyone who matched. Roy was awfully good at keeping secrets, and it took me quite a while to uncover all that I found."

"You did a remarkable job of it," I said, meaning every word of it. "But I'm curious about something. Did you just uncover all of this, or did you know some of it before we came by the office yesterday afternoon?" Her answer would be quite telling, no matter which one was true. If she knew so much before Moose and I came by, then she'd held out on us, but if she'd found out in the interim, that meant that she must have found some kind of diary or journal afterwards. Roy didn't strike me as the type of man who would record his thoughts on paper, but then again, I'd been wrong before.

"I knew quite a bit of it before," she admitted, "but I wasn't sure how much I could trust you with the information. Like I said, though, I asked around, and several people in town told me that I could count on you."

"We thank you for your faith," Moose said. "Did you share any of this information with the sheriff?"

"I tried, but he didn't seem all that interested in my speculations, so I finally just shut up. I had the distinct impression that he didn't like me."

I knew that Sheriff Croft liked to keep a bit aloof when he questioned folks he considered suspects, so I was sure that was what Kelly had experienced. It was interesting to me that Kelly made his suspect list, but then again, I could see how he might believe that her working for Roy and putting up with the man on a daily basis for seven years was plenty of motive for murder.

"I'm sure he was just doing his job," I said.

"I have a question for you, Kelly," my grandfather said. "Who do *you* think killed your former employer?"

"Honestly, it could have been any one of them," she said as she frowned. "It's sad, isn't it?"

"What's that, the fact that Roy was murdered?"

"Yes, of course there's that, but I mean the idea that so many people wanted to see him dead. I'd hate to think that you'd be able to come up with a list like that if something ever happened to me."

"Did you ever hear Roy mention anyone named Loretta Jenkins?" Moose asked in passing.

The secretary/receptionist frowned in concentration, and then she shook her head. "No, not that I can think of right offhand." After a moment's pause, Kelly asked, "Could that be the L.J. he had an appointment with last night?"

"It would make sense if it were," I said. I wasn't ready to tell her that Loretta claimed to be Roy's daughter. Springing it on her might come in handy later.

"Could you describe her for me?" Kelly asked.

"She's a petite woman in her early thirties with jet-black hair and brown eyes," I said.

Kelly looked at me curiously. "Are you sure?"

"That's as good a description as I can give," I answered. "Why?"

"Well, I don't know her name, but that sounds exactly like the woman I told you about earlier that's been stalking Roy for the past two weeks. I wanted to call the sheriff, but Roy wouldn't let me. She *has* to be the same woman."

"It wouldn't surprise me in the least," Moose said.

"The police should *definitely* talk to her, then. She made me nervous every time I spotted her nearby."

I was about to respond when my earlier fears were realized. I didn't know if it was merely coincidence, or if it was by plan, but when I saw the sheriff walk into the diner, I knew that it didn't matter one way or the other.

All that really counted was that Moose and I were busted.

"I didn't expect to find the three of you chatting at this time of day," the sheriff said as he approached us. It was clear that it was a direct jab, and given the circumstances, I didn't know that I could blame him.

"Kelly just dropped in all on her own for a cup of coffee and a chat," I said. "We were honestly surprised to see her visiting the diner."

Kelly looked at me a little oddly as she said, "I didn't realize that my absence here in the past was all that big a deal."

The sheriff stared at her a moment, as though he were analyzing the situation. "Let me get this straight. You came in here of your own free will, is that right? No one called you and invited you, did they?"

"No, I did it on my own. Why, does it matter?" She looked confused by the line of questioning, which just added to our credibility.

"Not really," the sheriff said. "Do you mind if I pull up a chair and join you?" As he asked it, he did as he'd threatened and started to sit.

"Actually, there's no need. I have to go," Kelly said as she abruptly stood. "I forgot all about it, but there was someone I was supposed to meet earlier, and I'd hate for them to think that I stood them up. What do I owe you for the coffee, Victoria?"

"Today, for you, it's on the house," I said. After all, it was the least I could do after she went out of her way to add to our knowledge pool.

"Thank you. That's most gracious of you."

After she was gone, the sheriff said, "You know, I don't think Kelly likes me very much."

"Then the feeling must be mutual, because she doesn't think you like her, either," I said. "As a matter of fact, she just told us that you intimidate her."

"What else did she happen to tell you while she was here?" the sheriff asked.

"Are you fishing for information?" Moose asked.

"Well, I hate to be picky about it, but in a way, you are still on my time."

Moose just shrugged. "It seems to me that you could drop a few nuggets our way as well. It's not asking all that much, when you consider how much we've been giving you lately."

I wasn't at all sure that my grandfather was handling things the proper way, but the sheriff surprised me when he smiled. "You make a good point. Okay, here's something interesting that I just found out. The poison used in your cake was just on Roy's piece. The lab analyzed the rest of it, and it was all clean."

"What kind of poison was used?" I asked. "Can it be traced in any way?"

"I'm afraid not. It was just common rat poison," he said. "It's probably in a hundred basements and garden sheds around town, and the chemical makeup is so generic that there's no way in the world to track it back to the owner unless we find a box of it at one of our suspects' places, and unless we get more of a reason to ask for a warrant than that, we aren't even going to be able to look."

"We might be able to handle that for you ourselves, unofficially, of course," Moose said.

"I'm going to pretend that you didn't just suggest that," Sheriff Croft said.

"That's fine with me, but does that mean you don't want us to do it, or you'd just rather not know ahead of time?" Moose asked.

"Breaking and entering, even if it's only a storage shed, is never acceptable as a form of investigation," he said stiffly. "Frankly, if I thought I really had to explain that to you, I would never allow either one of you near another murder investigation as long as I was sheriff. Do we understand each other?"

"Hey, it wasn't my suggestion, so don't scold me," I said.

Moose shook his head. "That's the way to show a united front, Victoria."

"If there's anyone in town who doesn't know that I've always got your back, they must be living under a rock, Moose."

My grandfather patted my hand. "Not only do I fully realize that, I greatly appreciate it."

"I'm glad we got that settled. Now, if you two will excuse me, I've got to follow up on a few more leads while I still have time to do it alone," the sheriff said. "Unless there's something else you would like to share with me."

I nodded. "Get out your notebook, because Kelly just told us a ton of stuff that she said she never mentioned to you."

After Moose and I brought him up to date, the sheriff nodded as he closed his notebook. "There's some good information there." He started to get up, but then abruptly sat back down again. "I'm going to tell you something else that isn't public knowledge, but it *is* a matter of public record, if you know where to look. I'd appreciate it if you didn't let anyone know how you found out about it, though."

"We are both the souls of discretion," Moose said. How he did it without smiling broadly was beyond me.

"Okay," the sheriff said. "It turns out that Mayor Mullins isn't nearly as wealthy as he likes folks to believe. His family fortunes have taken a substantial turn for the worse in recent years, and the amount he lost in his deal with Roy Thompson was just about enough to push him over the financial edge."

"Well, well, well," Moose said. "That's interesting

indeed." My grandfather looked at his watch, and then he smiled broadly.

"Why does that make you so happy?" the sheriff asked him.

"It doesn't, at least not specifically."

"Then why are you grinning like a hyena?" he asked.

"It's noon, Sheriff. That means that your suspect list is now officially fair game."

"I knew that I'd probably have reason to regret the deal I made with you two yesterday. I just didn't realize that it would happen so quickly."

"Don't worry. We won't do anything we shouldn't," I said.

"Victoria, you shouldn't make promises that I have no intention of keeping," Moose said with a broad grin. "Sheriff, we've shown you time and time again that we can be a real asset to your investigations. You need to trust us."

"I do, in my own way, or I wouldn't be here right now," the sheriff said as he stood. "All I can say is that you should both be careful, and happy hunting."

"Right back at you," Moose said.

After the sheriff was gone, my grandfather looked at me. "So, what do you say? Are you ready to get started?"

"Let me grab something to eat first," I said. "I've got a hunch that we're in for a long afternoon, and I don't want to face it on an empty stomach."

I expected a little resistance from my grandfather, but I was quite pleased when he said, "That's a sterling idea. Let's have your husband whip us up something quick and filling, and then our stomachs won't be rumbling with hunger when we start interviewing suspects."

"Did you have anything in particular in mind?" I asked as I started for the kitchen.

"No, why don't we just let him surprise us?"

"I'm game if you are," I said.

After we told Greg that we wanted quick bites, he made us grilled sandwiches that fit our preferences. I had a simply delightful ham and provolone cheese sandwich grilled perfectly, while Moose had Greg's wonderful chicken salad. My husband also ladled out bowls of soup for each of us. I got Greg's homemade chicken noodle soup that had never been anywhere near a can, while Moose got Greg's chili that he loved so much.

We pulled up a few stools in the kitchen as we ate so we wouldn't be in the way of Ellen and Martha as they took care of our customers. Greg barely listened to our strategy session as we ate, and it appeared to me that he was just happy having us as company. I worried about him working mostly by himself at the grill in the kitchen while everyone else was out in the dining room, but he didn't seem to mind. In fact, I think that overall, he was pleased with the situation. Working back there, Greg had the advantage of having the folks he loved nearby, and he could catch an occasional glance and hear a word here or there, all the while maintaining his own domain in back.

It made him happy, and that, in turn, gave me great joy.

It was so perfectly lovely back there that I almost hated leaving him and going out into the real world, but Moose and I had no choice.

It was time to start interviewing more people in order to find the killer who had tainted one of my husband's finest creations and used it to kill a man.

Chapter 9

"How should we handle this?" I asked Moose as we parked in front of Sylvia Jones's place near Molly's Corners. It was a pretty stately manor on the outskirts of town, with a long and winding drive that went past an expansive pond with a freshly painted gazebo perched on its edge.

"I think we should hit her head on," Moose said. "Let's not beat around the bush. Let's ask her for an alibi straight away."

"You always were one for the direct approach," I replied.

"Hey, it's been known to get results in the past," my grandfather said with a grin.

"Sure, but we've also gotten kicked out of a few places before the engine of your truck even had a chance to cool off."

"You've got a point. What do you suggest?"

"Well, she did just lose her ex-husband, no matter how she felt about the man. Why don't we start with our condolences and see where that gets us?"

"Okay, that might just work," Moose said. "If we're going that route, you can take the lead."

"Wow, did I seriously just win that easily?"

"Hey, I can bend when I need to," he said.

I decided to leave that one alone since I'd gotten my way.

We approached the massive front doors, and I rang the bell.

Before anyone answered, Moose looked around and asked, "What do you suppose they pay in property taxes every year on this place?"

"I can't imagine," I replied as the door opened.

I'd heard rumors that Sylvia had a butler on her staff, but I'd never really believed it. If this refined older man dressed in a suit was on her staff, I'd have a story of my own to tell

when I got back to the diner. "May I help you?" he asked
gravely.

"We're from Jasper Fork, and we came to offer Sylvia
our condolences," I said.

Moose nodded solemnly behind me, and I was hopeful
that he was indeed going to let me handle this interview,
though I knew that his decision to let me lead could change at
any second.

"I'm sorry, but Ms. Jones is not receiving visitors at this
time." He spoke with ultimate authority, as though his word
required immediate acceptance with no room for discussion.

"I completely understand," I said. "It's just that we feel
that it's important that she knows that the citizens of Jasper
Fork are feeling her loss as well. After all, Roy was a
cherished member of our community."

I could see Moose's eyebrow shoot up out of the corner
of my eye, but I hoped that the man acting as a gatekeeper
didn't.

"Who is it, Peter?" a woman's voice asked from inside
the home.

"Mourners," he replied.

"Show them in," she said after a moment's hesitation.

If Peter was surprised to hear the news, he didn't show it.
"Please, come in."

As he stepped aside, Moose and I walked into a grand
foyer behind him. There was a massive staircase centered in
the space, and a chandelier hanging down that must have cost
more than our diner. Sylvia Jones was wearing an elegant
black dress as she approached us, and so help me, a black
lace veil covered her face, though just barely.

"We're so sorry for your loss," I said as Peter discreetly
left the room.

Sylvia nodded. "Though it's true that Roy and I parted
ways many years ago, the man was never far from my heart."

Wow. That was giving their divorce a spin that any New
York PR flak would be embarrassed to try, but Sylvia pulled
it off without a moment's hesitation. This woman was going

to be more formidable than I originally thought.

"Had you seen him recently?" Moose asked. I had to give my grandfather credit. It was a pretty subtle way of finding out just when she'd last seen her ex-husband.

"As a matter of fact, we spoke on the telephone yesterday," she said.

So, that put her in touch with him the day he was murdered, but it wasn't what Moose had asked her.

"How about in person?" I asked.

"I'm not certain, but it had to be several days ago," she said. "While it's true that our split was less than perfect, we'd begun to grow closer over the past few months. I'm just sorry someone took the opportunity for us to reunite away from us."

I was going to need hip-waders if she kept this up. No one had whispered a word about Sylvia and Roy being anything but bitter enemies, but here this woman was trying to convince us that they were on the road to reconciliation.

"What's with the get-up, Mom?" Asher asked as he walked through the door without waiting to be announced. He was tall and thin, with sharp features and tight little brown eyes. "Come on. Are you seriously going to try to play 'grieving widow'? I doubt anyone who knows you is going to buy it." He seemed to notice us for the first time. "And who exactly are the two of you?"

"I'm Victoria, and this is my grandfather, Moose," I said. "We've met before, actually."

"Sorry, but I don't remember you," he said dismissively, and I didn't doubt it was true for an instant. I was pretty sure that I wasn't the kind of woman who ever made it onto Asher's radar.

"We run The Charming Moose," I said. "Surely you've heard of our diner in Jasper Fork. As a matter of fact, I'm certain that I've seen you around the place, and recently." This was my way of asking him if he'd been standing outside the diner earlier when Kelly had come by.

He started to say something, and then changed his mind.

"You're mistaken, because it doesn't ring any bells." What a lie that was. It appeared that the son was much like the mother, and I doubted that I could trust either one of them.

Sylvia recoiled when she heard me identify our diner. "Asher, these are the people who killed your father." Her features hardened as she asked us, "You've both got a lot of nerve showing up here. What are you *really* doing here?"

I knew I had to keep my voice calm and level in light of the accusation. It was tough, but I took a deep breath, and then I said, "Well, first of all, it's important that you realize that we didn't harm your ex-husband, and second, we already told you why we came. My grandfather and I wanted to tell you that we were sorry for your loss." I turned to Asher and added, "We're so sorry about your father."

"I don't doubt that you are, since your cake is what killed him, but save your sympathy for someone who cares."

"Asher!" Sylvia said harshly. "You mustn't speak that way."

"I refuse to rend my clothes over our loss, Mother," he said. "Take off that ridiculous outfit, would you? Roy Thompson didn't do us any favors in his entire life, and neither one of us owes him a second of mourning. He was never much of a father to me; we both know that, and there's no sense in pretending otherwise."

"It sounds as though you and your father had some real issues," I said. "When was the last time you spoke to him?"

Sylvia hadn't presented too difficult a challenge when we'd asked her in a roundabout way about the last time she'd seen her ex, but Asher wasn't buying any of it. "Is that your not so subtle way of asking me for my alibi yesterday? What business is it of yours?"

It was clear I needed to match his tone, or we were never going to get anything out of him. "You said it yourself. Someone used our cake to kill your father. We need to find out who did it so we can clear our diner's name."

I wasn't certain what I was expecting, but Asher's sudden smile caught me off-guard. "Okay, now that I can understand. Self-preservation is an excellent motivation to nose around into something that isn't any of your business."

"So, then, you'll give us your alibi?" Moose asked.

Asher's smile never broke. "Nice try, but no, that's not going to happen. I've learned that I rarely go wrong when I keep my mouth shut." He turned to Sylvia and added, "And I suggest you adopt the same policy yourself, Mother."

"Actually, she's already spoken to us about your father," I said.

That finally managed to break Asher's grin. "What did you tell them?" he asked. Before she could respond, he added quickly, "Never mind; we can discuss it later."

"Asher, there's no reason *not* to tell people our alibis. After all, we were together for the entire morning yesterday. Since we didn't go anywhere near that cake, we are above suspicion."

He *really* didn't like her telling us that. "Mom, would you mind if I borrowed your Jaguar? Mine's in the shop."

"Certainly," she said. "Let me just get you my keys."

"Thanks, I appreciate that." He waited until his mother had left the room when he turned to us. "Thanks for coming by, but it's time for you both to go now."

"I understand," I said. "After we say good bye to your mother, we'll be on our way."

Asher wasn't having any of that, though. "I'll be sure to convey your message."

Moose looked at me, and I could see the question in his eyes without him having to say a word. He wanted to know if we should push back and stay, or allow ourselves to be ushered out.

After a moment of thought, I shook my head slightly. There was no use getting on this man's bad side.

As Asher walked us out the door, I said, "I look forward to seeing you again soon. You really should come back by the diner sometime."

"How can I go back if I've never been there before?" he asked, and then closed the door between us.

"That was one of the slickest bum's rushes I've ever been given," Moose said. "I've got a hunch that the son is quite a bit more formidable than the mother. That particular apple didn't fall far from the tree, did it?"

"I'm not so sure that Asher's the one running things. I had a hunch that Sylvia was playing us all along," I said. "If you ask me, she could be more devious than her son."

"Maybe so, but either way, we're going to have a hard time cracking those two nuts."

I nodded in agreement as I said, "At least we finally got to speak with two of our suspects."

"Sure, but next time, I want to tackle them alone," Moose replied.

"You're not doing anything without me," I answered firmly.

"I didn't mean by myself," Moose said. "I meant separately. We should really try to split them up if we're going to do any good. We might be able to trap Sylvia if she's still trying to sell her 'grieving widow' act, and if it's just Asher, he might just be too clever for his own good."

"Okay, that all sounds good," I said. "I just hope we figure out how to do it. Did you notice that I put the emphasis on we?"

Moose laughed a little as we got into his truck. "You don't have anything to worry about. I wouldn't do anything without you, Victoria, and you know it."

"Well, it doesn't hurt to remind you now and then," I said with a smile of my own.

"Got it," Moose said as he started the engine. "Where should we go now?"

"Since we're in Molly's Corners, why don't we go ahead and try to see James Manchester again," I said. "Do you think there's a chance he'll agree to see us?"

"I've got an idea that might help accomplish that," Moose said.

"Care to share it with me?"

"Let me play with it while we drive, and I'll let you know

if it's any good when we get there," my grandfather answered. I didn't know if he was being coy, or if he really hadn't fully formulated his idea yet. Either way, I decided to respect his request, and we were mostly silent on the drive to James Manchester's office.

When we got there, Moose parked the truck, but I turned to him before he could get out on his side. "Okay, I was patient, but that's about all gone. What's our plan?"

"I think a mysterious hint that we know more than we actually do is our best bet," Moose said. "If we leave things vague but menacing, we might just earn ourselves a direct audience with the man."

"This ought to be good," I said. "It's your turn to take the lead, and to be honest with you, I'm looking forward to seeing it. Good luck."

He grinned at me as he tapped his temple. "With this brain, who needs luck?"

"Us, maybe?" I asked, and then I couldn't keep my laugh contained.

He just grinned, and then my grandfather said, "Doubt me if you will, but just watch the master at work."

"I'm looking forward to it," I said as I followed Moose inside. The office was nice enough, but there was nothing that shouted this man was one of affluence. In fact, it was all rather common, from the generic paintings on the wall to the slightly used furniture. Was it all some kind of smokescreen, or did James Manchester have less assets than we'd all been led to believe?

There was an older woman sitting at the receptionist's desk, and there was nothing flashy about her.

"May I help you?" she asked.

"We need to speak with your boss," Moose said.

"In regard to?" she asked gently.

"Murder," Moose said succinctly. I waited for him to embellish his statement, but he simply stood there looking down at her, as though he had some kind of right or authority to be there.

She finally realized that he was finished talking. The receptionist picked up her phone, whispered something into it, and then said vaguely, "Have a seat, please."

After we took up positions by the office door, I looked at Moose and nearly asked him if this was the sum total of his grand plan when he caught my eye and shook his head slightly. Okay, we were going to play this silent and mysterious.

I could do that.

Nine minutes later, I was ready to tell Moose that it had been a nice try, but he really needed to come up with something else, but I held my tongue. I knew that my grandfather had a great deal less patience than I did as a general rule, and if he could take it, then so could I.

Four minutes after that, I was beginning to have my doubts when the receptionist picked the telephone up again unbidden, whispered something else into it, and then hung up, offering us a quick frown as she did so.

Thirty seconds later, James Manchester came out through the door.

"Sorry to keep you waiting," he said, though for one second, I'd caught a hint of surprise in his glance. "Come right back."

We followed him through the dividing door into the heart of the office. This had been decorated more recently than the outer space, with a substantially larger budget. Fine leather chairs were nestled on a lovely and expensive rug, and the desk was mahogany. After we were all seated, Manchester said, "I'm surprised to see you both this far away from the diner. Delores tells me that you were quite melodramatic when you first came in. You gave her more excitement than she's had in years."

"There wasn't anything special about what we said," Moose replied. "It was true, though. We're here to talk to you about murder."

"Don't be a fool, Moose. I didn't kill Roy Thompson. Why would I?"

"Come on, we heard you threaten him ourselves," I said.

"If you recall, I didn't see him yesterday in his office. It turns out that was *after* the man was already dead, or did you choose to blank that part out?" Manchester asked. "Think about it. If I'd been the one who poisoned him, wouldn't *I* know that he wouldn't be in his office when I barged in there?"

"It could have all been a clever ruse to throw the police off your trail," I said.

James Manchester chuckled at that. "Trust me, I'm not that clever."

"You *were* at the celebration earlier in the day, though, weren't you?" I asked.

"Maybe I stopped and looked around on my way to Roy's office," he admitted. "I checked out the food, a few of the craft tables, and listened to the band. I didn't see Roy, though, or your cake either, for that matter."

"How could you have missed it?" I asked. "We had it set up on the square."

"Who knows? Maybe I did see it, but if I did, it never registered with me. Surely you have more than that to come in here accusing me of murder."

"Who was accusing you of anything?" Moose asked quietly. "We said we wanted to discuss murder with you, not accuse you of it."

"Delores must have misunderstood," Manchester said.

"You have to admit that you were pretty upset when we saw you yesterday, James," Moose said.

"That? I was just blowing off a little steam. Roy and I did a few deals together in the past, but this was the first one that lost me money. I was going to yell at him a little, he'd shrug it off, and then we'd move onto our next deal. You can't worry about every penny when you're investing as much as I do."

"It still can't be easy losing some of it," Moose said. "I know that I feel the pinch every time one of my stocks goes down."

"If you can't afford to lose it, you shouldn't be gambling with it," he said expansively. The telephone rang at that moment, and Manchester picked it up and held a whispered conversation. After a few moments, he hung up and grinned at us. "Apparently the first string is here."

"What are you talking about?" I asked.

"Sorry, I tend to use sports analogies when I talk. Sheriff Croft is here to ask me a few questions. I'd offer you the chance to go out the back way, but we don't have one."

I doubted that it was true, but I wasn't about to call him on it. "We're fine seeing him. The sheriff knows exactly what we're doing," I said.

"Then this shouldn't be a problem for anyone."

I stood, and Moose followed. "Not at all," my grandfather said.

Sheriff Croft's eyebrows shot up for a moment when he saw us in James Manchester's office, but he didn't say anything at first.

"Sheriff," Moose said as he waved two fingers at the man.

"Would you two mind hanging around outside for a few minutes?" the sheriff asked. "I shouldn't be long, and there's something I'd like to discuss with you."

I pointed to my watch. "We've been most careful with the time."

He shook his head. "That's not it. Something's come up, and I thought you should know about it. I won't be long."

Moose and I left, and as we walked out of the office, I suddenly turned and found Delores watching us carefully. She looked away the second that she realized I'd seen her, but it was too late. Evidently, we'd sparked some interest from the woman. Or was she just doing her employer's bidding by keeping a close eye on us?

"What do you think he wants with us?" Moose asked once we were out by the truck. "That was clever how you got that dig about the time into your response without giving anything away."

"I've been known to be crafty when the occasion called for it," I said. "As to what he has to say, I don't have any more idea than you do."

"Then there's not much we can do but wait for him out here, is there? It seems like that's all we're good for lately," Moose said.

At least the sheriff was as good as his word. Twelve minutes later, he came out the front door of the office, and based on the expression on his face, the interview hadn't gone exactly as he'd hoped that it would.

That didn't bode well for my grandfather and me.

Chapter 10

"I'm guessing that didn't go as well as you'd hoped it would," my grandfather said before I could get a word out on my own. "Manchester thinks he's above all of this, doesn't he? He treated us like we were some kind of joke."

"That man can talk five minutes and not say a thing," the sheriff said as he leaned forward over the truck-bed, planting his elbows on the frame of it. I'd seen it done a thousand times. A great many men from the South never spoke face to face. They all seemed more comfortable leaning against some part of a pickup truck, their eyes rarely making contact. "Every time I've tried to pin him down about an alibi, he manages to say a whole lot of words that don't add up to much."

"Well, if it helps," I said, "we saw him in Roy's office not long after he was poisoned. He was extremely upset with the man. I guess he could have been acting, but if he was, if fooled me. He admitted that he walked around the fair a little before he got to Roy's office, but he claimed that he didn't see Roy, or the cake, for that matter."

"Thanks, I appreciate that," Sheriff Croft said. "That was more than I managed to get out of him. He mostly just talked me around in circles."

"I'm guessing that's how he treats his business partners, too," Moose said. "Can you imagine him in a room with Roy Thompson? That's about as odd a couple as you'll ever want to see."

"I've got information that they did three deals together, but it's kind of odd," the sheriff said.

"What's so odd about it?" I asked.

"The first two deals they made together generated a good amount of income for Manchester, doubling his investment both times. The third deal, the latest one that just blew up on him, cost him all that he'd earned plus every dime he'd invested before, and another ten grand of fresh money thrown into the mix."

"Do you think Roy Thompson might have set him up?" Moose asked.

The sheriff shrugged. "I don't have any proof one way or the other, but if I had to guess, I'm willing to bet that old James in there got his clock cleaned by a professional. It appeared that he was under the impression that he was the shark in the deal, but I've got a hunch that he was wrong."

"I thought James Manchester was rich," I said. "He could afford to lose that kind of capital, couldn't he?"

"I don't think affording it had anything to do with it," the sheriff said. "You've met James Manchester, so you must have an idea of what he's like, and from what you told me, you saw him pretty steamed yesterday in Roy Thompson's office. Did he seem like a man who would take losing *anything* with a whistle and a smile?"

"Not a chance," Moose said. "Is that why you wanted us to hang around, to talk about James Manchester?"

"No," the sheriff said with the hint of a smile. "Part of it was just out of pure meanness. I wanted you both to cool your heels a little while I did a little investigating."

I shrugged. "But just a part of it, right?"

"Just a part. There's been a development I thought you both might like to know about."

That got my attention. Since when was the sheriff so interested in actively sharing information with us? "We're happy to get any help you feel like giving us," I said.

"My team has been checking folks who had cameras or cell phones who took pictures at the celebration yesterday," he said. "That was one of the reasons we spoke to so many people after Roy was murdered."

"That's absolutely brilliant," I said, meaning every word of it. Why hadn't Moose or I thought of that? It reminded me that, as good as my grandfather and I were at digging into murder, Sheriff Croft was certainly no amateur.

"Is that sarcasm, Victoria?" the sheriff asked, his voice suddenly hard.

"No, sir, it is open admiration. Did you have any luck?"

He appeared to accept the compliment, and then he shrugged. "We got the scene with you and Roy on film from some high school girl's video phone. She seemed to think that it was pretty hilarious."

I was suddenly embarrassed yet again about the way I'd acted. "Why would she want to tape that?" I asked.

"She didn't start out filming you. Her mother was at home sick with the flu, and she wanted to see what was going on at the festival, so her daughter took some video of the square. She was filming when she saw you and Roy, and we've got pretty good visual proof that you didn't dose that cake with rat poison while it was in your possession. If you did it, you managed to fool all four cops who've watched the video."

"At least that's good news," I said, though I must not have showed much enthusiasm.

"Funny, but I thought you'd be a little happier about us clearing your name," the sheriff said.

"I'm happy enough about it, but then again, I already knew that I didn't kill Roy, so all your proof does is clear me from your suspect list."

"I didn't say that," the sheriff said.

"Do you mean to tell us that Victoria is *still* a suspect in Roy's murder?" Moose asked, clearly not believing it any more than I did.

"No, not really," Sheriff Croft admitted. "Honestly, I never thought she did it in the first place. It was just nice getting that video as confirmation so I could convince anyone else if I had to."

"Did you come up with any other evidence with all of those photos and videos?" I asked the sheriff.

"Well, we've got some random shots on the square that put some of our other suspects there at the crime scene."

"Care to share any names with us?" I asked.

"I'm not so sure that would be prudent just yet," the sheriff said.

"We're not asking to see the pictures," Moose said. "But a hint or two wouldn't hurt our investigation, and remember, we're sharing everything we learn with you as soon as we realize that it might be significant. Sheriff, we've proved ourselves over and over again. There's no reason in the world you shouldn't trust us."

"I guess it's just habit," he said. "Okay, I'll tell you, but none of this is to be repeated. Do we understand each other?"

"We do," Moose said, and I nodded my agreement as well.

"Okay, so far, we've got shots of James Manchester, Hank Mullins, Asher, and another woman I'd like you to identify, if you can. But first, do either one of you care to comment on any of the names that I just mentioned?"

I thought about it, and then I told him, "Manchester and Mullins have already admitted being at the celebration, but the fact that Asher was there is new information. When we spoke to his mother, she claimed that she and her son were together the entire time her ex-husband had been poisoned."

"How did you manage to get her to admit that? Every time I've spoken to her, Asher won't let her say a word until he vets it first."

"We were lucky enough to catch her alone," I said. "She was pretty free in telling us both that Asher was her alibi."

He nodded. "I might be able to make that work later, then. Thanks for the information. Now about that photograph. Why don't you both take a look at it, and tell me if she looks familiar to either one of you." The sheriff reached into his shirt pocket and pulled out a single photograph. I took it from him and looked at it as Moose leaned over my shoulder.

I instantly handed it back to the sheriff, and he looked disappointed by my reaction. "Well, it was a long shot."

"I didn't have to look at it long to know who it was.

That's Loretta Jenkins." The image had been a little blurry, and Loretta was turned partway from the camera, but there had been no doubt in my mind upon seeing it.

"Are you talking about the woman who's been going around claiming that she's Roy Thompson's daughter? Are you sure? Both of you?"

Moose and I both nodded. "There's no doubt in our minds. How did you know to pull that photo out of the pile in the first place? Was it from the description of her that we gave you?"

"I admit that it rang a few bells when I saw it, but what really sealed the deal was the man who took it. He said he was trying to get a shot of her to show Roy Thompson."

"Why would he do that?" Moose asked.

"He used to work for Roy, and he noticed that she was following him around the entire time he was in the square. He figured he might be able to sell his old boss the information when he decided that she was up to no good."

"Wow, Roy really didn't inspire much loyalty, did he?" Moose asked.

"I don't know if you can say that."

"Why's that?" Moose asked me.

"Look how long Kelly Raven worked for him," I replied. "Seven years is a long time."

"I've been wondering about that, myself," the sheriff admitted. "From what I've heard, he was an entirely unpleasant man to work for, and yet she was with him all those years. Did he pay her that well, or was there another reason she stuck around?"

"What could that possibly be?" I asked him.

"I don't know, at least not yet, but it's interesting enough to make me want to find out. Do you two have anything else for me from your activities since noon?"

I thought about it, and then shook my head. "Sorry, but that's about it."

"How about you, Moose?"

My grandfather shrugged, and then he said, "You know

as well as I do that we just got started digging into this with free access to the suspect list. You've got better resources, and you've had more time to dig into it. I was kind of hoping that you'd have something else for us."

"Sorry, but there's nothing that I'm ready to share," the sheriff said. As he headed back for his squad car, he said, "Keep in touch, okay?"

"You do the same," Moose said, and the sheriff drove away.

"Where do we go now?" I asked. "Should we try to talk to Mayor Mullins again since we're in town, or should we try to track Loretta down?"

"Let's swing by the mayor's office. You know how I hate to backtrack."

We got to the town's offices, but unfortunately, the mayor wasn't all that interested in seeing us.

"Do you have any idea when he'll be free?" I asked Helen Parsons.

The earlier version of her was gone, replaced by a woman who appeared to have forgotten how to smile. "I'm afraid that he's tied up, and most likely he will be for the rest of the day. You could always try again tomorrow."

I looked at Moose, and then I jerked my head subtly toward the woman. Where was the charm now?

"Helen, I hate to impose, but this really is important," Moose said in that cajoling voice of his.

She didn't give the slightest flicker of acknowledgment that we'd even been there before. "Actually, it's Ms. Parsons, and I'm sorry, but I can't help you."

Moose frowned, and then my grandfather turned to me as he said, "Thank you for your time. Let's go, Victoria."

Once we were outside, I asked, "What was that all about?"

"I'm guessing that His Honor wasn't too pleased with how she dealt with us before."

"He must have really raked her over the coals. She barely made eye contact with either one of us."

Moose just shrugged. "I never claimed to be a miracle worker. What do you say? Should we go on and head to Laurel Landing?"

"I don't see any reason why not," I said. "There's nothing left here for us to do at the moment."

As we walked to where the truck was parked, I said, "It really bothers me that Loretta just dropped off the face of the planet like that. I wonder where she is."

"Victoria, do you think there's the slightest chance that she might have killed her father, and now she's in hiding?" Moose asked me.

"I don't even know for sure if Roy Thompson really *was* her dad," I answered.

"I've got a hunch that she's going to need more than a simple blood test to prove it," Moose said. "Can you imagine Asher giving up a nickel of his father's inheritance without a fight?"

"I can't even see him sharing anything with his mother, let alone a stranger who shows up claiming to be his half-sister," I said.

"Oh, I have a hunch that she's not going to have any problem fighting to prove that she's a rightful heir as well."

"Like father, like daughter, I suppose," I said.

"So, where does that leave us?" Moose asked.

"Well, we now know that Asher was at the celebration, and if what Sylvia told us was true, she had to be there, too, since she claimed that they both alibied each other. That means that either one of them had the opportunity to lace that cake with poison," I said, "but then again, so did James Manchester, Hank Mullins, and Loretta Jenkins."

"Who else does that even *leave* on our suspect list?" Moose asked.

"Just Kelly Raven. If she was at her desk all morning like she claimed, then it would clear her of murder."

"I don't even know about that," Moose said. "It might be pretty hard to prove that she was there all morning, since she was supposedly alone. Then again, that rat poison doesn't act instantly, from what I've read about it. She could have dosed him with it before things even got rolling on the square."

"But she still couldn't have gotten it into the cake unless she was there at the celebration," I said. "Remember? That's where they found traces of it when they analyzed the sample."

Moose nodded. "Good point. That had slipped my mind. That's why we're such a good team, Victoria. Between the two of us, we have one good brain."

"I hope we have more than that," I answered with a smile as we got to Moose's truck. "We can't rule Kelly out as a suspect based on what we know so far."

"I just hope that we have more luck in Laurel Landing than we've had around here," Moose said.

"I can't think of any better place to dig, and while we're there, I've got someone else I'd be interested in talking to, if we can find him."

"Who's that?" Moose asked, a troubled expression creeping up. "You're not holding out on me, are you?"

"No, but remember when I first spoke with Loretta, she mentioned living with a boyfriend in Laurel Landing? Surely she told him about her rich father. What if he decided to help her out and make sure that Loretta got her share of the estate sooner, rather than later?"

"That's an excellent point," Moose said. "But how are we going to find him? We don't even know his name."

"I admit that it won't be easy," I said, "but that doesn't mean that we shouldn't at least try."

"I agree," he said. "Let's backtrack later if we have the time and give it another shot trying to speak to the mayor. Right now, though, I feel like Loretta is a much better lead at the moment."

"Let's go," I said.

We'd been on the highway for less than twenty minutes when I looked back over my shoulder for the third time since we'd gotten back in the truck.

"You're going to strain your neck if you keep doing that," Moose said.

"I can't shake the feeling that someone is following us. Have you noticed that black sedan four cars back?"

Moose adjusted his rearview mirror trying to see the car, but clearly he didn't catch it. "I don't see any black sedans," he said.

"It was there, I tell you," I said.

"I believe you, Victoria, but it's got to be a coincidence. This is the easiest way to get from Molly's Corners to Laurel Landing. It wouldn't surprise me if all of us were headed in the same general direction."

I looked back again, but if the car was still tailing us, I couldn't see it. "Never mind. It was probably just the result of my overactive imagination."

"There's no crime in that," Moose said. "After what happened to Roy yesterday, I think we're all entitled to be a little jumpy, don't you?"

"Maybe you're right," I said. I looked back twice more, just in case, but the sedan was gone. Either the driver had realized that we knew he was tailing us and dropped out, or he'd arrived at his destination without a single thought about my grandfather or me.

As we pulled into Laurel Landing, I asked Moose, "Do you have any ideas how we might be able to find Loretta or her mysterious boyfriend?"

"Well, we're not without resources here, are we?"

I thought about our earlier visits to Laurel Landing when we'd investigated murders before, and two places came instantly to mind. We'd made friends with a local attorney named Monica Ingram, and Moose had gotten reacquainted with the owner of the BBQ Pit, a man named Charlie. I'd met two waitresses who worked there, Josephine and Stacy, but I wasn't all that certain that either one of them would welcome a return visit from me. I'd suspected both of them as possible murderers earlier, and my questioning hadn't been entirely welcome. Hopefully, neither one carried a grudge, but I had a hunch that Moose and I were about to find out.

"Why don't we stop off at Monica's office first?"

"We'll probably have better luck at the barbeque place," Moose said.

"You're still intimidated by Monica, are you? She's perfectly harmless. Actually, I'd say that she's quite nice."

"To you, maybe, but then again, we both know that she's not my biggest fan."

"Moose, is there ever any chance that you'll grow up and get over this?" I asked. Monica was perfectly lovely, but there was something about her that intimidated my grandfather, and that was something that not many folks could claim.

"I suppose that I could, but then again, what fun would that be?" he asked as he pulled into the law office's parking lot.

I got out, and then I leaned back in before I shut the door. "I want you to promise that you'll stay right here until I get back. No wandering off, and I mean it."

"Yes, Ma'am," he said with the hint of a smile. "I'll be here."

"Good," I said with a smile. "Thanks for doing this."

"Hey, I've got nothing to lose by hanging around," Moose said, and as I walked toward Monica's office, I glanced back and saw that he'd already buried his nose in a crossword puzzle. My grandfather believed that puzzles kept his mind alert and agile, and I wasn't about to dispute it. I liked them myself.

I pulled open the front door and walked in, only to find more of a day care than a law office inside. The girl behind the desk had a baby laid out on a large pad, and she was in the middle of changing a diaper.

"I'm so sorry," the girl said, looking quite flustered. "No one's due in for an hour. This must look really bad."

"Don't worry about it," I said as I offered her my hand

without thinking. "You must be Lisa. Monica's told me all about you."

She looked at my hand, and then at hers. "Honestly, it's probably better for both of us if we don't shake hands."

I knew that Monica wanted to keep her secretary no matter what it might cost her, and I wasn't about to botch the deal if I could help it. "Is your boss anywhere around?"

"She's in court," Lisa said. "You won't tell her that you found us like this, will you? I really need this job."

"From what I've heard, you both need each other. Don't worry about me; your secret is safe."

"Thanks so much," Lisa said as she finished diapering her child. The used diaper went into a discard bucket with a clever lid on it after she put her baby back in the nearby crib. I recognized it from the last time I'd been in. Monica had been assembling it, and now that there was a baby in it, I hoped that she'd done a good job.

"It's fine. I'll talk to her later," I said as I started for the door.

"You could always leave her a note, if you'd like," Lisa said.

"Just tell her that Victoria came by," I answered.

Her face lit up a little at the sound of my name. "So, *you're* Victoria. Monica told me that you were someone worth knowing, and I can see that she was right."

"It's kind of her to say so. I happen to think you're pretty lucky having a boss like her."

"Believe me, you're not telling me anything that I don't already know," Lisa replied. "She was so sweet to hold my job for me."

"I have a hunch that it was her pleasure."

Lisa smiled as I said it, and then she turned back to her baby. "Justin, I know that expression on your face. Are you doing what I think you're doing? I *just* changed you."

I wasn't about to hang around to find out just what Justin was up to.

I walked back to the truck, and Moose frowned as he

looked over my shoulder. "What were you expecting to see?" I asked him as I got in and buckled my seatbelt.

"What I didn't want to see was your attorney friend. Did you get a chance to speak with her, Victoria?"

"No, she's in court," I said.

As he started off toward the BBQ Pit, Moose said, "It took you an awfully long time to determine that."

"I had to wait for her secretary to finish changing her baby's diaper before I could ask about Monica," I admitted.

"Are you telling me that she's keeping a baby in the outer office?"

"Come on, it's not like it's some kind of wild animal," I said with a smile. "Lots of people have babies in their offices."

"Lots? Really?" Moose asked skeptically.

"Okay, maybe not lots, but I'm sure that some of them do."

"Fine, some offices have babies in them. Did the new mommy happen to say when Monica was getting back?"

"She's in court, so who knows how long that might be," I said. "Most likely, we won't need her anyway. After all, we've still got our diner sources, don't we?"

"We do," Moose said as he pulled into a spot in front of the BBQ Pit and shut the truck engine off. "Why don't you tackle the waitresses, and I'll handle Charlie."

"You know that I'm perfectly capable of questioning the owner myself, don't you?" I asked.

"We both know that you're *more* than capable of it," Moose said, "but if we want any answers that mean anything, I'd better be the one asking the questions. Charlie might tell something to another old coot that he wouldn't say to a young gal like you."

"Are you calling me young just to get your way?" I asked him with a grin.

"No, not at all. It's just that when you're compared to me or Charlie, you're *bound* to be the youngest one in the group."

"I'll give you that," I said. As we walked in, I spotted Stacy waiting on tables. She was working the room alone, and I wondered where Josephine had gotten off to. Was she on break, was this her day off, or had she left the BBQ Pit altogether? I knew that she and Stacy worked their shifts at the diner together, though the two women seemed to have trouble getting along with each other most of the time.

As Moose started for the kitchen to find Charlie, I walked straight toward Stacy. "Hey there. Long time, no see," I said.

"Victoria, what are you doing here?" Stacy asked with a smile as she balanced a tray overloaded with pulled pork barbeque, baked beans, hush puppies, and cole slaw. I followed her to a nearby table, and as she distributed the contents of her tray, she said to me, "I'm surprised to see you during regular working hours. Did you close up your diner just to come see us?"

"My grandmother's subbing for me on the job right now," I said. "Where's Josephine? She didn't leave you, did you?"

"Are you kidding? That woman's never going to leave this place. She's just taking time off to recover from a little bit of surgery."

"Is something wrong?" I asked with concern. While it was true that the woman and I hadn't gotten along all that well earlier, I still didn't wish that kind of problems on her.

"Don't worry; it's nothing serious. If you ask me, she's milking it for everything it is worth. It's being all kinds of overblown around here," she said loudly enough for Charlie to hear her in the back with no problem.

"How long will she be out of work?" I asked.

"Two more days," Stacy replied. "Listen, I've got another order up, but after that, I've got a few minutes, if you need them."

"That would be great," I said.

"Can I bring you anything while you're waiting?" she asked me with a mischievous grin. "You know that you at least want a sampler plate."

I'd had a sampler before just to be agreeable, but I'd fallen in love with the Pit's offerings with that first bite. "Well, maybe a small one," I said.

"I'll have Charlie fix you right up," she said.

I knew that I was going to regret the calories, but what I wouldn't regret was eating the heavenly food in the first place. The smoke ring alone on the bark of the barbeque was enough to make my mouth water, and I found myself thinking more about the pulled pork than I was about the murder case. By the time Stacy came back, I was ready to eat the countertop in front of me.

The first bite was every bit as good as I remembered it to be, and the sweet tea was sugary enough to set off alarm bells ringing in my head.

In other words, it was all perfect.

"So, was there a reason you and your grandfather stopped by?"

"We're looking for someone," I said after biting a hushpuppy in half and feeling the rich cornmeal explode in my mouth.

"Anybody in particular?" she asked me as she reached for a pitcher of sweet tea nearby and topped off my glass, even though I'd had only two sips so far.

"There's a young woman who lives in town named Loretta Jenkins. She's evidently staying with her boyfriend, but I don't know his name, or where to find either one of them."

"That's okay," Stacy said as an angry expression bloomed on her face. "I know him well enough for both of us. He happens to be my brother, and if you ask me, the two of them deserve each other."

MOM'S HOMEMADE CHICKEN POT PIE

We love this pot pie, and serve it year-round. It's especially nice when you have leftover chicken, or turkey, for that matter. I used to make my own crusts, and you can still do that if you'd like to, but this is a go-to meal when I don't feel like going to much fuss. It might be noted that we also enjoy the tang of cranberry sauce with this meal. Don't worry, the canned variety is just fine. A side of butter beans are the final touch in our household, but feel free to skip them entirely, since there are already plenty of yummy veggies in the pie itself.

Ingredients

4 Tablespoons butter, unsalted
4 Tablespoons flour, all purpose, unbleached
2 dashes table salt
2 dashes pepper
1 ¼ cups milk (2% or 1%)

mixed vegetables, frozen mix (12 to 19 oz) (We like the blend with corn, peas, carrots, and green beans, but the size depends on your pie dish and how much veggies your family likes)

1 pie crust, from the frozen section for a quick meal, or made from scratch if you're feeling adventurous.

For scratch crusts only:
1/3 cup lard
1 cup flour, unbleached all purpose
1 dash salt
3-4 Tablespoons water

Directions

Preheat the oven to 425 degrees F.
Next, in a large pan, melt the butter over low heat. While the butter is melting, defrost the veggies in the microwave, and if you're using a store-bought crust, let that rest on the counter at room temperature now. When the butter is melted, remove the pan from the heat and add the flour, salt, and pepper, mixing it all together until it's incorporated. Put the pan back on low heat and cook this flour/butter mixture for 2-3 minutes, stirring repeatedly. Next, add enough milk (3-4 Tablespoons) to the pan to make a smooth mixture. Stir this constantly, still on low heat. When the mixture is smooth, add the rest of the milk and turn the heat to high, stirring constantly. When the first bubble forms, remove your pan from the heat altogether and continue stirring. Add your frozen veggies now, mix them all in thoroughly, and then transfer the mixture into an 8 or 9 inch pie pan. Cover it with a store-bought crust (or the handmade one you made ahead of time), pinching the edges and cutting slits in the top of the crust to let steam escape during the baking process. Gently wash the top with egg white for a shinier crust if desired before it goes into the oven.
Bake in the 425 degree F oven for 25-35 minutes, or until the crust is golden brown. Take out and serve!

Author's Note:
Sometimes I like to make smaller one-serving portions using bowls that are oven-safe. These can be festive during the holidays, when I also tend to get a little fancier with the crusts, making lattice patterns or cutting out sections of the dough with small cookie cutters before baking.

Handmade Crust Directions (optional)

In a small bowl, work the lard into the flour/salt mixture with a fork until you form pea-sized pellets. Next, sprinkle in water, one tablespoon at a time, and work that into the pastry. Add more water in one teaspoon increments until the mixture pulls away from the side of the bowl and the flour is incorporated into the dough. Be careful not to add too much water too quickly, or you'll have a gooey mess on your hands. When you're happy with the results, form the pastry into a ball, flatten it with a rolling pin to ¼ to ½ inch thickness, and then proceed with the directions listed above.

Chapter 11

"Don't you and your brother get along?" I asked Stacy.

"He's a bum, a drunk, and an ex-con who uses people and throws them away like they're soiled paper towels," she said. "The second he got out of prison, he and Loretta got together, even though I warned her that she was ruining her life. She says she loves him, and she must if she's willing to put up with what she has for his sake."

"Why was he in prison, if you don't mind me asking?"

"I don't mind a bit. I washed my hands of him well before that happened. Steve gets mean when he's drinking, and a man was foolish enough to cross him when he had a full load on. Steve beat him up pretty good, and it took three cops to pull him off. He was sentenced to nine years in prison for aggravated assault and a bunch of other charges, and we all kind of got used to the peace and quiet around here. Then they decided that he was a model prisoner, and it wouldn't hurt to let him out early. He served seventeen months of a nine-year sentence. That's early, all right. He keeps saying that he's changed, but I'll believe it when I see it."

"Do you happen to know where he is right now?" I asked.

"He's at his job; at least he is if he knows what's good for him. His parole officer will send him back in a heartbeat, all he needs is a reason, and Steve's too smart to do anything that stupid. At least he has been so far."

"I'm really sorry. I didn't mean to bring up bad memories for you. That seems to be the only way we talk, doesn't it?"

"It's not your fault, Victoria," Stacy said as her hard expression softened, if only for a moment or two.

"Trouble does seem to follow me around," I admitted. "Where does Steve work?"

"He repairs tires over at Al's," Stacy said. After a second, she added softly, "Don't tell him that I told you where he was, okay?"

"Stacy, are you afraid of your brother?"

"You would be, too, if you'd seen the man he beat up," she said.

"I promise that I won't say a word to him about you," I promised her.

"I appreciate that."

I was about to ask her for directions to Al's when Moose came out with Charlie. "Stacy, if you've got a second, my friend here would like to speak to you."

"That's okay. We've already covered it," I said. I slid a twenty under the plate, as much for the information as the taste of wondrous barbeque. "Keep the change."

Stacy didn't fight me on it, and I had to wonder if she considered it hazard pay for the information that she'd just given me. If that was the case, I was afraid that Moose and I were going to have to have a little chat before we tackled Steve. My grandfather tended to shoot from the hip, and I didn't want to take a chance on anything happening to him during one of our interviews. We were going to have to tread lightly when we spoke with the ex-con.

I just hoped that my uncle was up to the challenge of keeping his own temper in check.

"You're a hard woman to track down," I said as we found Loretta in back of the tire place. She was bundled up and sitting in a folding chair reading a magazine, and the woman looked genuinely surprised to see us.

"How did you know where I'd be?" she asked.

Before I could answer, Moose said off the cuff, "We were driving by, and I wanted to get a price on some new tires for my truck. It was pure chance that we both saw you back here when we got out."

"Well, I don't sell tires, but they do in there," she said as she pointed to the front.

"This is kind of an odd place for you to be hanging out," Moose said.

"I'm waiting for my boyfriend." She glanced at her watch, and then added, "He gets off work in twenty minutes."

"How nice for you," I said. "While we've got you here, I was wondering if we could ask you something."

"Sure, go on. Ask me anything. I've got nothing to hide," she said as she continued to flip through her magazine.

"Did you speak to your father yesterday at the celebration before he was murdered?"

Loretta's face clouded up. "I told you that I was in town, but I didn't say anything about being anywhere near the celebration. What makes you think that I spoke to him?"

"We were going through some photographs earlier, and your face popped up near him in one of them," I said.

"Who was showing you pictures of me?" she asked, clearly not happy about this new development. It was obvious that Loretta liked to be in control of whatever situation she was in, and she was quickly losing control of this one.

"The sheriff had quite a few photographs from the celebration, and he asked us to help him identify several people he didn't recognize," I said.

"You told him who I was, didn't you?" Her voice was calm as she said it, but somehow, it was one of the scariest things I'd ever heard in my life.

"Be reasonable, Loretta. We had no choice," Moose said.

"I'm sorry that you did that," Loretta said coldly.

"What did they do?" a burly young man asked as he came out of one of the nearby garage bay doors. He was wearing a gray and red Al's uniform, and from the roughly executed tattoos on his arms, it wasn't tough to guess that this was Steve, the ex-convict Stacy had told me about. He was handsome in a disheveled kind of way, and he held a greasy rag in one hand and a tire iron in the other.

"We were just talking," I said.

"About what?" he asked, getting between us and Loretta.

"These are the people I told you about who are investigating my dad's murder. Guess what? They told the police who I was," she said.

"That wasn't the brightest thing to do," Steve said as he frowned. "You both should have kept your noses out of this."

Moose stood his ground, refusing to back down one step. "Let's not forget that your girlfriend came to us for help in the first place. She asked us to find out who killed Roy Thompson, and we can't do that without the police. Think about it. If we didn't tell them who she was, they would have found out on their own, and they wouldn't have been happy about it. By telling them first, we stay in their good graces, and that gives us access to more information so we can figure out who killed Loretta's father."

"What you should be worried about is staying in *my* good graces," Steve said, not buying my grandfather's argument.

I was proud to see that Moose didn't even flinch. "That's where you've got it wrong. We want to know the truth; to be honest with you, we don't care who murdered Roy Thompson as long as we find out who did it. Our cake was used as a murder weapon, and we're not about to let the killer get away with that. At least you know what our rationale is. Has it been your experience in the past that the police have such lofty motives?"

He spat on the ground. "The cops just want an easy answer. They don't care if it's the right one or not."

"So then we're agreed. We'll keep helping Loretta, but only if she is willing to cooperate."

The man frowned, clearly wondering how things had reversed so quickly, and I marveled yet again just how charming my grandfather could be when he set his mind to it.

"Yeah, I guess that just makes sense," Steve said.

"Hey, don't let them off the hook that fast, okay? They were asking me if I killed Roy when you came out," Loretta protested.

"That's not entirely true," I said. "We just need to know if you spoke to him yesterday before he was murdered. If you did, perhaps he told you something that might help us, or maybe you noticed him talking to someone. That's information we could use, too."

"I never said a word to the man in my life, and that's the honest truth," Loretta said as she broke eye contact with me. It was usually a pretty good indication that someone was lying to me, but this wasn't the best time to call her on it.

"What about the pictures we saw? You were standing pretty close to him in the one the police showed us," I told her.

Loretta looked pained to admit it when she said, "I lost my nerve at the last second, okay? He had that blasted cake in his hands, and I was three feet away from him. If I'd had any idea that it was poisoned, I would have knocked it to the ground right then, but who knows? It might have already been too late to do him any good."

"What do you mean?" Moose asked.

"There was a bite already missing from it when I first saw him," she said.

"Think hard for a second, Loretta. Was that before he sat down, or after?" I asked.

"It had to be before," she said after a moment. "He was still walking around when I almost got my nerve up to approach him." She looked as though she was ready to cry at any second by the admission, and really, who could blame her? She'd waited too long to meet her real father, and that hesitation had killed any chance she might have had to have a relationship with him.

"It's okay," Steve said in a surprisingly gentle voice as he moved closer to Loretta. "It wasn't your fault."

"I should have talked to him when I had the chance," she said, her voice faltering a little as she said it. "Now I'll never be able to introduce myself to him as his daughter."

"Is that all you need to know?" Steve asked as he looked at my grandfather. "Can't you see that you're upsetting her?"

"We're truly sorry for that," Moose said, "but these questions need to be asked, if not by us, then by the police."

"Will you tell them that she didn't do it? And if you do, what chance is there that they'll believe you? This is tearing her up." The hard man had gone soft around his girlfriend, and he was doing what he could to protect her.

"It would be best if she told them that herself," Moose said. "The sheriff's looking for her, and the harder he has to search, the worse it's going to be for everybody when he finally finds her."

"What do you suggest I do?" Loretta asked.

"If it were me, I'd go straight to the police station in Jasper Fork and let him interview me there. As a matter of fact, I've been the center of one of his investigations before, and that's exactly what I did," I said.

Steve seemed to look at me with new respect. "He actually accused you of murder?"

"Not formally, but then again, I didn't hide from him."

Steve appeared to consider that, and then he turned to Loretta. "I'm going to take off early. We need to go see this guy so we can get him off your back."

"I'm *not* going to the cops," Loretta said fiercely. "Whose side are you on, anyway?"

"I'm on yours; you shouldn't even have to ask," Steve said. "Do you think I like this any better than you do? I'm sorry, but it sounds like this is the best choice we've got."

"I've got all those traffic and parking tickets," Loretta protested. "He's going to arrest me for them if I walk into the station no matter what."

"Can you do anything about that?" Steve asked me calmly. "It would really help if we could work that out beforehand. If this guy gives us his word that he won't arrest Loretta for those tickets, can we believe him?"

"You can. If he goes back on his word, you can take it up with me."

Steve thought about that, and then he said, "Go ahead,

then. Call him."

"I'll do my best," I said. Moose nodded in agreement, so I got my cell phone out.

"Sheriff, I need a favor," I said, not trying to soften my end of our conversation. I wanted them to know that, at that moment, I was on their side.

"I don't have time to do anything for you," he said gruffly. "I've been trying to track this Loretta Jenkins down all over Laurel Landing, and so far, I'm coming up empty."

"You're still in town?"

"I am, for what little good it's doing me," he said.

"What if I could promise you an interview with her in the next five minutes?" I asked.

"Go on, I'm listening."

"Loretta's worried about her outstanding parking and traffic tickets," I said. "She's afraid if she speaks with you, you'll arrest her on the spot."

"What does she expect me to do, tear them all up if she cooperates with my investigation? I'm not making a deal like that with anybody, Victoria, and frankly, I'm surprised that you'd even ask me to."

"You don't understand. She doesn't expect you to make them go away. She just doesn't want you to lock her up because of them."

"I don't care one bit about any of that," he said. "I'm trying to solve a murder here. I won't get rid of the tickets for her, but I won't arrest her because of them, either."

"We have your word on that?" I asked, and then held the phone out so that everyone could hear his response.

"You do."

"That's good enough for me," I said. "We're in back of Al's Tires right now. Do you know where it is?"

"I'm two minutes away. Don't any of you go anywhere." He hung up, and I turned to Loretta. "I held my phone away from my ear. Did you hear that? He gave his word."

"We heard," Steve said. "Now I just hope that his word is good."

"I guarantee that it is," I said.

"Then you'd better hope he keeps his promise," Steve said.

"I won't tolerate threats against my family," Moose said coolly.

"I wasn't threatening you," Steve said. "I'm not like that anymore."

"What changed?" I asked.

"I stopped drinking. I was a mean drunk, and I got what I deserved. I'm putting that all behind me now, with Loretta's help. If I'm a little defensive and act a little tough, that's just what prison does to you."

Sheriff Croft showed up less than two minutes later as he pulled up in back of the tire shop. As he got out of his cruiser, he nodded to Moose and me, and then focused on Loretta. "You're a hard woman to track down."

"She didn't do anything wrong," Steve said.

The sheriff glanced at him, and apparently he knew in a heartbeat that Steve had spent some time behind bars. "Who are you, and why is it any of your business?" he asked, his voice flat and without inflection of any kind.

"I'm her boyfriend," Steve said.

"Congratulations. Now, wait over there with them until we're finished."

It was pretty clear that Steve didn't like being ordered around, and I was afraid for a second that we might have an ugly incident on our hands, but after a moment's hesitation, he did as he was ordered.

"This guy's got an attitude problem," Steve mumbled as he approached us.

There was nothing that I could say to that, so I decided to keep my mouth shut. Besides, I wanted to hear the sheriff interview Loretta Jenkins. Who knew? Maybe I could pick up a tip or two along the way.

"Let me get this straight. You claim to be Roy Thompson's illegitimate daughter, is that right?" the sheriff asked.

"I am," Loretta answered simply.

"Can you prove it?"

"My mother told me that it was the truth, and I have no reason to doubt her," Loretta said a little defensively.

The sheriff smiled slightly, but then he quickly buried it. "I understand how you must feel, but I'm looking for something a little more concrete than that."

"What do you want, a birth certificate or something? I can tell you right now that my mother left that entry blank."

"I was thinking more along the lines of a DNA test," Sheriff Croft said.

"I'd be happy to submit to one," Loretta said. "Bring it on."

The sheriff jotted something down in his notebook, and then he asked, "Tell me the last time you spoke with the victim."

"Could you not call him that?" Loretta asked. "He was a normal person, just like you or me."

The sheriff shrugged. "Okay, when did you talk to Roy?"

"Actually, I never spoke to my father," she said.

"If it helps any," I said from a distance, "she told us the same thing earlier."

The sheriff gave me one withering look, and I shut right up.

"But you were seen near him yesterday at the celebration," the sheriff said. "As a matter of fact, we have visual evidence of it."

"You don't have a picture of the two of us talking," Loretta said, "because it never happened. I tried to approach him, but I lost my nerve at the last second."

"Tell him about the cake," I said.

Again, I got a dirty look, and I decided to try to really focus on not saying anything else for the rest of the interview.

"What about the cake?" Sheriff Croft asked reluctantly.

"He ate some of it before he sat down," she said. "Does that mean anything?"

"I don't know yet," he said.

"Am I free to go now?" Loretta asked. "I've told you everything I know."

"Oh, I have a few more questions," the sheriff said with a smile that I doubt he felt. "It's better to get these over with right now, don't you agree?"

She looked at Steve, who nodded in agreement, though it was clear he was reluctant to agree. "Fine, go on and ask away," Loretta said.

Twenty minutes later, Sheriff Croft flipped his notebook closed. "Thank you for your cooperation."

"That's it? We're finally finished here?"

"Unless something else comes up," he said. To my surprise, the sheriff didn't head for his cruiser, but instead, he walked directly to Steve.

"Where did you do your time, and what were you in for?" he asked Steve.

He told him, and then he added, "Sheriff, I paid my debts. I know where I went wrong, and I'm not about to go back in. Not for anything."

"Where were you yesterday between nine and one?" he asked.

"I was here working," Steve said. "If you don't believe me, feel free to go ask my boss."

"Will he tell me that you were here the entire time? What about your lunch break? How long do you get?"

"Yesterday two other guys were out sick, so I didn't even get to eat my sandwich until two. I worked on a dozen cars, right out there in plain sight."

"We'll see," the sheriff said as he closed up his notebook and then headed into the shop.

"Will your manager back you up on your alibi?" I asked.

"You bet he will," Steve said with the first hint of a grin we'd seen out of him. "He was on my case the entire time, and I seriously doubt that he went five minutes all day without yelling at me to hurry up. I was pretty steamed about it at the time, but it worked out, didn't it?"

"You have an alibi, but it doesn't do me any good," Loretta said. "I was there when he was murdered."

"Don't worry. They'll clear you," he said as he pointed to Moose and me.

I didn't know when he'd developed so much confidence in us, but it wasn't in my best interest to argue him out of it. "We'll do our best," I said.

Loretta clearly looked unhappy about the close grilling she'd just gotten. "That man thinks I did it. I just know it," she said.

"He treats everybody that way. Trust me, you're not his only suspect," I said, trying to reassure her, but Moose sent me a warning glance that told me I should drop it.

Loretta wasn't interested in that, though. "Really? Like who?"

"The police don't share everything with me," I said, and I saw her hopeful expression start to fade.

"That's what I figured," she said.

"I have one more question for you myself," I said.

Loretta looked as though she were at the end of her rope. "Give me a break, will you? I'm sick of answering other people's questions."

"Just one," I said.

"Fine. What is it?"

"You had an appointment with your father last night. What was it about?"

"What makes you think I had an appointment with him?"

"We saw his schedule," Moose said.

"It wasn't the first one I made," Loretta said. "I cancelled twice before. I kept losing my nerve, you know?"

"What did you say it was about when you called?" I asked.

"I made something up, okay? What does it matter now? The man's dead. He's kept the last appointment that he's ever going to." Loretta glanced into the tire store and saw that the sheriff was talking to another man, presumably the owner. "Listen, I'm not hanging around here so your friend can change his mind about locking me up." Loretta started to leave, and then she glanced back at her boyfriend. "Are you coming, or what?"

"I'll be right with you," Steve said, and then he turned to me. "If you need anything, and I mean anything, no matter how rough it might be, call me here and leave a message. I'll get in touch with you."

"What exactly are you proposing?" Moose asked.

"Hey, I can make people cooperate who aren't in the mood to change their minds. It could come in handy, and I'm not squeamish."

I'd heard enough of that. "Thanks for the offer, but I think we'll be fine on our own," I said.

"Steve, come on," Loretta barked at him, and he shrugged.

"There's no talking to her when she's like this," he said as he trotted after her. Coming into this encounter, I had been under the impression that Steve was some kind of evil influence over Loretta, a man who might be capable of taking things into his own hands, but he said he was trying to change, and I believed him. It might be easy enough for the homicide to be pinned on him if he'd been at that fair, but his alibi was solid. Loretta, on the other hand, was a study in contradictions. She claimed to be in mourning over her lost father, but that hadn't affected her self-preservation instincts one iota. There was a hint of tenderness in her, but I had a hunch that there was a great deal more of the pragmatist in her when it came to being suspected of murder.

Chapter 12

"What do we do now?" I asked Moose after we left the tire place. The sheriff hadn't even come back to speak with us after he confirmed Steve's alibi. So much for earning a little gratitude for arranging the meeting with Loretta.

"There's not much else we can do," Moose said. "I say we go ahead and start back toward the diner."

I stood there thinking about the possibilities, and then I said, "I think we should head back to Molly's Corners instead."

"Any reason in particular?" he asked me.

"I want to take another swing at the mayor," I replied.

Moose grinned at me as he asked, "Do you mean that figuratively, or are you going to actually punch him?"

"We're not there yet," I said. "I'm just frustrated by the man's refusal to see us today. We both know that there was no meeting earlier. He just didn't want to have to deal with us."

"I can't imagine why not," Moose said with a smile. "After all, doesn't everyone like to be considered a murder suspect?"

"I know firsthand that it's not all that pleasant an experience, but we have a right to talk to him, don't we?"

"I don't know about a right to do it, but it would be nice if we could have another chat and ask him about his finances, I'm willing to admit that much. Victoria, do you really think that it will do us any good? After all, I haven't met a politician yet who didn't think that lying was their fallback position."

"You don't mean that, do you?" I asked.

"No, of course not. I can be cynical at times, but even I'm not that bad." As we got into his truck, he said, "I don't have anywhere else I need to be if you don't. Let's go see what our mayoral friend is up to."

"I wouldn't call him our friend," I said.

"Neither would I. It was just a figure of speech."

When we got to the town hall parking lot in Molly's Corners, I spotted a car parked in the lot and veered toward it.

"Where are you going?" Moose asked.

"This is the mayor's car," I said as I approached. Even though it was a chilly day, when I touched the hood of the car, it was still warm. The sun didn't account for it either, since the day was decidedly overcast. "The hood's still warm," I said.

"So? That just means that he's been out."

"I knew I'd seen this car before. Moose, this is the car that followed us to Laurel Landing. I'm sure of it."

He frowned at me, and then my grandfather looked at the car again, as though it had its own secrets to share with us. "Victoria, there must be a thousand cars like this registered in the state of North Carolina. The only thing distinctive about it is the fact that we're looking at it right now."

"It could have been him, though. Are you at least willing to admit that much?"

Moose shrugged. "I suppose so. If it's true, what does it mean, though? Why would the mayor refuse to see us, and then follow us to another town?"

"If he's guilty of murder, he probably wants to know what we're up to in our investigation," I said.

My grandfather seemed to ponder that for a few moments, and then he said, "I suppose it's possible, but even it if it's true, how does it help us?"

"Moose, if he's the killer, we can focus more of our attention on him."

My grandfather shook his head. "That's an awfully big if, Victoria, and you know it."

"Maybe so, but he fits the bill as a potential killer, doesn't he?"

"So do all of our other suspects," Moose reminded me. "I'm not willing to declare him guilty yet and be done with our investigation without a whole lot more proof."

"Okay, but I'm planning to keep an eye on him."

"I would expect nothing less of you," Moose said.

Unfortunately, if the mayor was indeed in his office, we weren't going to be able to speak with him, at least not today.

"If we can't see him right now, then I'd like to make an appointment for the first thing tomorrow morning," I said when Helen Parsons told us that we weren't allowed access that day.

She tapped a few keys on her keyboard, stared at the screen, and then said, "I'm sorry, but he's booked up for the rest of this week and halfway into next. The soonest I can get you in to see him is next Thursday at four in the afternoon. Shall I put you down for that time?"

"No, thank you," I said.

Moose smiled at Helen as we left, but it didn't do either one of us a bit of good.

Out in the parking lot, I said, "I'm sorry. It looks like we came here for nothing."

"I wouldn't say that," my grandfather said. "In my opinion, it's more telling that he wouldn't see us than that warm car hood."

I brightened a little. "Does that mean that he goes to the top of our list?"

"He's close enough to being there already on his own," Moose said. "Why don't we discuss this on our way back to the diner?"

"That sounds good to me," I said.

As we drove, Moose said, "There's one good thing about all of this driving. It gives us a chance to talk about our list of suspects."

"I don't know. I kind of enjoy just hanging out with you," I said.

"Right back at you," Moose said. "So, should we get

started?"

I took a deep breath, and then I began assessing our list of our suspects, and how likely it was who the killer really was. "First off, we have to seriously consider Sylvia and her son, Asher. We know that at least one of them was at the festival, and if we can believe Sylvia, they were together the whole time."

"Do we know for a fact that Asher inherits Roy's fortune now that he's dead?" Moose asked.

"I don't even think *they* know for sure, but it's not a bad guess, if Roy believed that Asher was his only child."

"And I wouldn't put it past Sylvia to poison her ex-husband in order to insure her son's fortune. Loretta's thrown a wrench into those plans, but as far as we know, neither one of the them knew about her before."

"As far as we know is right," I said. "There's another reason one of them could have killed Roy. They may have wanted to knock him off before he could change his will to one more favorable for Loretta. That gives them another motive."

"If you look at it another way, it gives Loretta and Steve a motive as well. We just have Loretta's word that she and Roy never spoke, but what if she talked to him and told him that she was his daughter? If Roy rejected her, she might kill him out of spite, or pragmatically, before he could write something formally that she was disinherited. Plus, even if Steve can prove that he wasn't anywhere near Jasper Fork, we know for a fact that Loretta was there."

"Wow. So we have pretty solid motives, and opportunities, for three of our suspects," I said.

"And we're not even finished yet," Moose said. "Let's not forget the two men with business ties to Roy Thompson. It doesn't really matter how rich Mayor Mullins and James Manchester both might be, nobody likes getting cheated."

"And it sounds as though Roy duped them both," I added. "We saw how upset James Manchester was at Roy's office. Let's not forget that the mayor has been claiming that he could take the hit of losing money, but the sheriff and Kelly both discovered that Mullins doesn't have nearly as much money as he likes to claim around town. And speaking of Kelly, I have a few suspicions about her myself."

Moose looked genuinely surprised by that. "Do you honestly think that she could have killed her boss?"

"Why not? Could you have worked for that man for seven days, let alone seven years, without entertaining thoughts of killing him?" I asked.

"Nothing that I'd ever follow up on," Moose said.

"How do we know what Kelly's motivation might have been? If she did it, I'm sure that she had her reasons."

"It just doesn't make sense, though. She could have poisoned him any day of the week," Moose protested.

"Sure, but then the suspicion of his murder would fall directly on her. Think about how much more clever it was to wait until lots of other people had a chance to do it as well."

"Victoria, do we have any reason to believe that she had anything to gain by basically killing her golden goose? Without Roy, Kelly is bound to be out of a job soon."

I nodded. "Sure, but what I really want to know is if she's mentioned by name in the man's will. They worked closely together for seven years, and Roy wasn't all that close with anyone else. What if he left her enough so that she could afford to retire? It might not be a fortune in most people's eyes, but it could be motive enough for her."

"I'm getting tired of guessing. We need to get our hands on that will," Moose said.

"We can always ask Rebecca to look into it, but there's a good chance that it hasn't been filed yet, so there's no way for us to know."

"Was she his attorney?" Moose asked.

"I have no idea, but if it's been filed, she might be able to find out who his beneficiaries are."

"Then call her, Victoria. Knowing what he wrote in that will could go a long way toward figuring out who killed him."

"It's worth a shot," I said as I took out my phone and dialed Rebecca's number.

Fortunately, she picked up on the first ring. "Hey, it's me," I said. "Do you have a second?"

"Just about that," Rebecca said.

She sounded stressed out, and I hated to bother her. "This can wait. Just call me when you get a chance."

"No, I can talk, just not for long. What's up?"

"Moose and I are trying to find out if Roy Thompson's will has been filed with the probate court yet. Do you happen to know anything about it?"

"I heard rumors that he used an attorney in Charlotte, but when he files the paperwork, he'll have to do it in our county."

"Can you ask around and see if it's been submitted yet?"

"I'm due there myself on another matter in a few minutes," Rebecca said. "I'll call you if I find anything out. Sorry, but I really do have to run."

"Go," I said. "And thanks."

Unfortunately, she'd already hung up by the time I'd gotten my thanks out.

"She doesn't know, but she's going to look into it," I told Moose as I put my cell phone away.

"Rebecca's a good friend to have," Moose said.

"For more reasons than her connections at the courthouse," I agreed.

"So, is that it for our list of suspects?" Moose asked.

"Well, unless there's yet another mystery partner that we don't know about, that just about covers it. It's enough, though, don't you think? We have six pretty viable suspects, and any one of them could have killed Roy Thompson."

"So, we're pretty sure that it's one of the following people: Sylvia Jones, Roy's ex-wife; Asher, his estranged son; Loretta Jenkins, his illegitimate daughter; James Manchester and Hank Mullins, two of his scorned business partners; and finally, Kelly Raven, his secretary/receptionist. Does that about sum it up?"

"That's all that we know about," I said. "If Sheriff Croft has other names on his list, we don't know about them."

"If he does, he can deal with them himself. We already have more than we can handle with the names that we've got."

"So, the only people we've been able to eliminate so far without a doubt are the one ex-con we had as a suspect and our town's best barber. The rest of our suspects are supposedly honest and upright citizens. One of them's a mayor, for goodness sakes."

"That doesn't make him honest or upright," Moose said with a grin.

"I already know your opinion of politicians," I said with a laugh. "We can't let that influence us one way or the other, though."

"Agreed, though it's true that the man's been acting strangely when it comes to us."

"Who knows? Maybe he acts that way around everybody."

"I doubt he'd get reelected if he did," my grandfather said.

"Our list is the best we can manage to come up with at the moment given the information we have," I said as we neared the diner. "For now, I just want to finish my shift, and then go home and have a fire with my husband."

Moose looked up at the sky. "You'll have to have it in your fireplace inside. It's going to rain before you get off work."

I looked up, and while there were a few dark clouds in the sky, I had no idea what the weather might bring. "How can you be so sure? Are you basing that on just a few clouds?"

"That, and the fact that my leg is killing me. Whenever it hurts like this, it's going to either rain or snow, and I don't think it's cold enough for snowflakes. It will still be chilly, but it's going to be rain when it hits the ground."

"You sound pretty sure of yourself," I said as my

grandfather parked the truck in the back of the parking area we all used.

"I'll bet you ten to one that I'm right. You pick the stakes."

"No, thanks," I said. "I know you wouldn't be that bold if you weren't sure."

Before we made it to the front door, the first raindrops hit us both.

We dashed inside together, and I looked at my grandfather, who couldn't stop grinning.

"What's so amusing?" Martha asked when she saw her husband's face.

"Nothing much. I just love being right; do you know what I mean?"

Martha grinned. "We all know what you mean, Moose. Did you have any luck with your investigation?"

"It's too soon to tell," I said. I kissed her cheek, and then I said, "Thanks for watching the front for me."

"It was my pleasure," she said.

I smiled at Jenny as I walked past her, and Greg was happy to see me when I came back into the kitchen.

"Hey there," he said with a smile. "I missed you. Are we having a fire outside tonight?"

"I'd love to, but Moose just made it rain."

Greg looked puzzled by my statement. "I knew that he could do a remarkable number of things, but I didn't realize that he was all that proficient at rain dances."

"Well, maybe he didn't cause it, but he surely did predict it. I'm afraid we're going to miss our outdoor fire tonight."

"There will plenty of time for that later," Greg said as he hugged me. "After all, we've got the rest of our lives."

"Maybe so, but I wanted one tonight," I said.

"Then we'll light up the fireplace and snuggle under a blanket together. How does that sound?" my husband asked.

"Like we should close up now and avoid the rush," I replied with a grin.

He laughed, and then my husband released me. "Patience

is a virtue, my love."

"I know. I just don't feel all that virtuous at the moment."

I made my way back out front, and I found that Jenny had her hands full with our dinner customers. I jumped in and started helping out, glad that our diner's business hadn't completely blown away with Roy Thompson's death.

I did notice that not many folks were having dessert, though.

Chapter 13

"Is it too late to be calling?" Rebecca asked when I answered the phone at home later that night. "I kind of got distracted, and to be honest, I forgot all about calling you."

"That's okay. It's not even nine o'clock yet." Since I had to be at the diner before six just about every morning, I had to get to bed at a decent hour so I could get my beauty sleep. Otherwise, I tended to get kind of grumpy, and nobody was a fan of that, least of all our early morning customers.

"Okay. I'll make it quick. I just got back from having drinks with Roy Thompson's Charlotte attorney, a man named Paul Gray. He was at the courthouse at the same time I was there, and I happened to overhear what he was talking about, and we had a nice little chat."

"Is he attractive?" I asked instantly.

"Oh, yes. I didn't mind the assignment you gave me at all. There's a problem, though. He's just getting out of a long-term relationship."

"Don't let that stop you," I said with a laugh. "But what happened to the last guy you were dating? You didn't even want to tell me his name because you were afraid that it might jinx it."

"Well, it managed to get jinxed anyway. I'm sorry to say that he didn't work out," Rebecca said.

"Do you have any more details than that that you're willing to share now that's over? You know I live vicariously through you."

"Then I'd say that you have a sad and lonely life. You have to know that I'd trade you for what you've got with Greg any day of the week."

"And I'd turn you down every time you asked," I said. "So, tell me about Paul."

"That's not as important at the moment as what he told me about Roy Thompson's will," Rebecca said, "or more significantly, Roy's plans to change it completely right before he died."

"WHAT?" I asked loudly enough to get Greg's attention.

"Is anything wrong?" he asked me.

"No, it's just Rebecca," I said in a calmer voice. "Everything's fine."

My dear friend laughed when she heard me say that. "Since when did I become 'Just Rebecca'?"

"You know what I mean. What exactly did he tell you?"

"It was pretty amazing, to be honest with you. It turns out that Paul was heading to Jasper Fork yesterday as Roy Thompson was dying."

"Was he making a change that quickly?" I asked.

"Roy told him that he was completely revamping his will, and Paul even brought two people from his office to witness the changes, along with a notary to make sure things were taken care of immediately."

"Did he happen to mention how things were going to change, or is that not a fair question to ask?"

"Well, I think Paul was trying to impress me a little, so he probably said more than he would have in ordinary circumstances."

"Rebecca, did you take advantage of that man for my sake?"

I could hear the grin in her voice as she answered, "Let's just say that I was in the mood to be impressed. Would you like to hear what he told me?"

"You bet I would," I said. This was getting good.

"Okay. From what Paul told me, every last dime of Roy's money was going to go to a foundation for the preservation of historical landmarks. Everyone listed before was getting cut of their inheritance completely. From what I gathered, it's a pretty substantial amount, too."

"I didn't know that Roy Thompson was that fond of old buildings."

"He wasn't particularly, according to Paul. It was just his way of twisting the knife a little. It's a shame he never got a chance to do what he wanted to with his money."

"So, who gets it all in the old will, the one that's still valid?"

"Currently, it's split right down the middle," Rebecca said.

"Between Asher and his mother, right?" I guessed.

"Well, you got half of it right. Asher is indeed one of the beneficiaries. It's the other name he mentioned that surprised me."

"I give up. It wasn't his daughter, was it? I didn't think he even knew about her existence." That would certainly give Loretta incentive to knock off her old man.

"No, it wasn't his child, not unless he adopted Kelly Raven at some point."

"Are you telling me that Roy Thompson left half of everything he had to his *secretary*?" I asked, shocked to learn the new information. "Were they, you know, fooling around or something?"

"According to what Paul said when he told Kelly the news, she made it quite a point to stress that wasn't the case at all. He said that she seemed genuinely shocked when she found out."

"I bet she won't turn it down, though," I said.

"Do you know something about her that I don't?" Rebecca asked.

"It just seems kind of odd, if you know what I mean. Has he already filed the will with the probate court?"

"I have a hunch that *nothing's* going to happen with the estate while the two main beneficiaries are both murder suspects."

"How long can the court delay things?" I asked.

"It depends on how much pressure is applied on it not to process the will."

"I have a feeling the sheriff is not going to want to help a murderer collect a big payoff. Moose and I might still have a little time."

"I wouldn't drag my feet, if I were you. Asher's already making noises about expediting the entire process, and from what Paul said, Kelly's not fighting him at all."

"I wonder what Loretta is going to say when she finds out that she's being left out in the cold," I said.

"Are you going to tell her yourself?" Rebecca asked me. It was clear that she was hesitant about that happening.

"It's not going to put you in a jam if I do, will it?"

"If it does, it's nothing I can't handle," she said.

"But you'd rather I didn't say anything to her at all. Is that true?" I asked, pushing a little harder.

"You know what? You have my blessing to tell her anything you want to at all, Victoria. Just don't let her know how you found out. Will you do that much for me?"

"I won't say a word to her about anything. Your friendship is more important to me than any murder case."

"I appreciate that," Rebecca said, "but if you keep my name, and Paul's, out of it, that will be enough."

"Okay, if you're sure."

"I am," she said as she stifled a yawn. "Listen, I'm beat. I'll talk to you later."

"Bye," I said, "and thanks for going to such extreme lengths to get me that information."

"It was my pleasure," she said, and then, Rebecca added with a laugh, "and I mean every word of it."

After we hung up, Greg saw me start to dial another number. "You're not calling Loretta now, are you?"

"Were you listening in?"

"Shamelessly," he admitted with a grin.

"No, I thought I'd touch base with Moose before I did anything," I said.

"That's a good plan. What do you think this all means?"

"Well, I'm certainly going to start looking at Kelly Raven harder than I have been before. I'll tell you one thing; Moose is not going to like this."

"Why not?"

"He thinks that Kelly is too sweet to get her hands dirty with murder."

"With the motivation we know she had now," Greg said, "it wouldn't surprise me if she decided to speed up her inheritance and spread a little poison."

"I think it's possible, too."

Moose answered on the first ring. "What's going on, Victoria?"

"Were you waiting by the phone for me to call, Moose?" I asked with a smile.

"Well, I'm guessing that Rebecca called you. Do I have to beg, or are you going to share what you learned with me?"

"No begging required," I said. After I brought him up to date about my conversation with Rebecca, there was silence on the other end of the line. "Moose? Are you still there?"

"I'm trying to digest everything you just told me. We've got two suspects that just went to the head of the line, don't we?"

"Three," I said. "We can't sell Sylvia short. She could have done it to insure her son of what she must think of as his birthright."

"True, but if Roy told Loretta that she wasn't getting a dime of his money, she could have killed him out of anger instead of greed."

"So, the only ones we can eliminate now are the two businessmen who got skewered in their deals with Roy, is that how you see it?" Moose asked.

"No, they're still viable, too. This murder might not have anything to do with Roy's will."

"Then what good does it do knowing anything about who Roy was planning to leave his holdings to?"

"Moose, you know as well as I do that all we can do is collect information at this point. Who knows which particular piece is going to be the one that gives us the answer to the entire puzzle? You've got to keep the faith."

"It just gets frustrating sometimes, you know what I mean?"

"Oh, trust me, I know," I said. "I think that we should wait until morning to tell Loretta about her father's intentions to write *everyone* out of his will."

"He couldn't write her out if she was never there to start with," Moose reminded me.

"That's a good point, but I still want to see how she takes the news that she's not getting a dime of Roy Thompson's money."

"Let's do it together. I'll see you when you get off at eight tomorrow morning, and we'll tackle her first."

"That sounds great," I said, and then hung up the phone.

"I heard most of that," Greg said. "Moose is right. The new information really didn't do you much good at all, did it?"

"Not yet, but who knows what tomorrow might bring?" I asked.

My husband hugged me, and then he said, "I don't know, and as long as I get to spend at least some of it with you, I'm okay with that."

"So am I," I answered.

It was ten minutes after six in the morning when Loretta Jenkins walked into the diner, looking as though she hadn't slept an hour the entire night. If I had to guess, I'd say that someone had already told her about her father's will. I wondered who'd beaten me to it.

"Do you have a second?" she asked me as I helped Ellen wait on the first of our customers. We had a handful of regulars who never missed having breakfast with us, and one of the things they said they liked best about us was our prompt and friendly service.

"If you can give me five minutes, I can manage it, but right now I'm jammed," I said.

Loretta nodded, and then she pointed to a booth off to one side. "When you get a chance, I'll be over there."

"Can I get you something while you're waiting?" I asked.

"Coffee; black, and lots of it."

"Rough night?" I asked.

"You don't know the half of it," she said.

I had a hunch that I did, but I wasn't about to spoil the surprise if she was here because of something else entirely. After I helped Ellen with the crowd of customers we had, I walked over to Loretta. "Are you sure that I can't get you something to eat? It might make you feel better."

"After what I heard last night, I doubt that," she said.

"I don't know. My mom makes a pretty mean Denver omelet."

"You make your mother work in the kitchen at this hour of the day?" Loretta asked, a little unbelieving.

"That's nothing. My husband takes over when she goes home. When we say that this is a family business, we mean that everyone pitches in, even our mascot moose."

As I said the last part, I gestured to my hand-carved moose, but Loretta didn't even look in his direction.

"Whatever," she said. "My dear, sweet half-brother dropped a bombshell on me last night. He gets half of everything according to the latest will, and I don't get a dime."

"You don't say," I said, trying to hide the fact that I already knew. "Who gets the other half, if it's not you?"

"Some trollop that worked for him," Loretta said with clear distaste. "If they think that they're going to get away with this, they are sadly mistaken. I was up all night talking to Steve. He told me that I should just let it go, can you believe that? Just because my father and I never had a relationship is no reason that I shouldn't be one of his heirs, you know?"

"Well, I've never been in your position," I said as tactfully as I could. "I'm not quite sure how I would react if I were."

"Trust me, you'd want the money," Loretta said. "Do you know any good lawyers around here?"

"I might know one," I said. "Why do you ask?"

"I need someone on my side in this mess. I hear there's a

woman named Rebecca Davis in town. Is she any good?"

"She's the best," I said. "Are you sure there's no other way than litigation to work something out?"

"Hey, I never started this. I was willing to settle for something reasonable, but Asher just laughed when I suggested it. Now I want it all."

"But he has the will in his favor, isn't that right?"

"Who cares? Clearly our father wrote that before he knew that he had a daughter, too."

Maybe Roy did, and then again, maybe he didn't, but it wasn't my place to tell her that. Besides, how could I say a word now, since I hadn't disclosed it earlier? For now, I was going to have to go with the strategy I'd adopted of feigning ignorance. "Rebecca is an excellent attorney, but I should tell you up front, my recommendation isn't unbiased. We've been best friends forever."

"Can I trust your opinion about her skills?" she asked.

"I think you can, but how can you take my word for it that I'm telling you the truth?"

She just shrugged. "I need to trust somebody in this ugly business. Why shouldn't it be you? Where can I find this Rebecca woman?"

I glanced at the clock. "If I know her, she's still in bed. She doesn't open her office until ten."

"I'll get her up before that," Loretta said.

"She's not going to open her office up early just for you," I said. I was pretty safe in saying that, since my friend enjoyed her sleep more than just about anything else.

"When she finds out how much money she stands to gain if we win, she'll wake up, you can trust me on that. Is she in the book?"

I nodded. "She sure is; it's listed under R. Davis. Good luck."

"I don't need luck," Loretta said as she slid a dollar down beside her mug. "I have the truth on my side."

She might have thought so, but I had the feeling that even with Rebecca's vast legal skills, it was still going to be a lost cause.

Then again, I'd been wrong before.

Chapter 14

"Are you ready to roll, Victoria?" Moose asked as he came into the diner around eight, rubbing his hands together, just as he'd promised.

Martha kissed me on the cheek as he added, "I want to catch Loretta before she has the chance to duck out on us."

"I'm sorry, but it turns out that you're too late for that," I said. "She came by here a little after six this morning."

"Why didn't you call me?" he asked petulantly.

"Well, first of all, I wasn't about to wake you up, and second of all, there was no time. She was in and out during our first push of customers, and when I finally had a chance to chat with her, she left before we could get into anything significant."

"Did you tell her about Roy's will?"

"I didn't have to," I said. "Evidently Asher called her last night. She's going to fight him in court for a share of the inheritance, and she's trying to hire Rebecca to represent her."

"She could do worse," Moose said.

"That's what I told her. I'm sorry, but there was just no time to bring you in on it."

"That's fine," he said. "Did I come by for nothing, then?"

"No, I think we should go have a chat with Kelly right now."

"Do you honestly think that she bothered coming into work after finding out how much she is going to inherit from her boss? I doubt that I would, given those circumstances."

"We *both* know that's not true," I said. "Your worth ethic wouldn't let you skip out, not if you knew there were things that needed to be done."

"Maybe not, but how do we know that Kelly feels that

way, too?"

"There's only one way to find out," I said.

"Let's go, then."

"Thanks again for covering for me again," I told my grandmother. "I'm trying not to make a habit of it."

"You're doing something extremely important," she answered.

"So are you," I said as I hugged her on the way out.

Moose and I drove to Roy Thompson's office, and I was beginning to have my doubts that we'd find Kelly there. That fear was reinforced when I realized that the only vehicle parked out front was one that I didn't recognize. Moose and I walked in the door, and I saw a handsome man in his early forties dressed in a nice suit leaning over Kelly at her desk, studying a computer monitor. So, she was there after all.

"Sorry. We didn't mean to interrupt," I said.

"You're not," Kelly said as she automatically tried to scoot her chair away from the shadow of the man. It had the unfortunate consequence of striking him directly on the knee, though.

"Careful," he said with a hint of irritation in his voice before he turned to us. "May I ask what business you have here?"

"We came by to see Kelly," I said. I offered him my hand as I added, "You must be Paul Gray."

He took it, but frowned slightly as he did so. "How could you possibly know my name?"

"Rebecca Davis is my best friend," I said with a smile.

His frown vanished in an instant, replaced with more than the hint of a smile. "Rebecca's something, isn't she?"

I glanced at Kelly and saw that she was not at all pleased by Paul's change of attitude. Was she interested in the man herself? "She is first class all the way," I said.

"You must be Victoria," he said, and then he turned to Moose and offered his hand. "And I'm guessing that you're the famous Charming Moose."

"I hope that at least some of the things you've heard

about me are positive," my grandfather said with a grin.

"Some are," Paul said, matching my grandfather's grin with one of his own. I liked this man, and I was hopeful that something might work out between him and my best friend. "I'll give you all a little time to chat. I need to make a phone call to my office anyway."

The attorney left the room and went into Roy's space, and after he was safely behind closed doors, Kelly bit her lower lip. "I didn't know that he was seeing Rebecca."

"They're pretty new," I said. How new, I wasn't about to explain. "We understand that congratulations are in order."

"What? Oh, the money. I suppose so."

"Tell me that you're not excited," Moose said. "No matter how unfortunate the circumstances, you're a very wealthy young woman now."

"That might all be a bit premature," Kelly said, "but even if it were true, I'm not so sure I'm going to accept it. What was Mr. Thompson thinking, leaving me all of that money? And if I take it, what are people going to say?"

"Do you mean this wasn't just a reward for your years of loyal service?" I asked her.

"That sounds so ridiculous I don't even know how to respond to it. Do you know what my Christmas bonus was last year?"

"I don't have a clue," I said.

"He bought me a turkey. It wasn't even cooked. What was I going to do with a turkey? I live alone, and I don't eat meat anyway."

"What's your point?" Moose asked.

"If he cared that little about giving me something while he was still alive, why on earth would the man name me in his will?"

"So, are you saying that you didn't know this was coming?"

"I didn't have a clue. The first thing I thought when Paul told me about it was that he'd been drinking. Then I figured it was some kind of joke, but it's finally starting to sink in.

I'm not going to spend a penny until I know it's mine, though."

So it was Paul, was it? I'd have to give Rebecca a heads-up about Kelly's interest. "Have you heard about Loretta's intentions to take the estate to court?"

She nodded unhappily. "She made that point loud and clear when she came by the office this morning before Paul got here. I have half a mind just to give her my share and be done with it."

"What's keeping you from doing exactly that?" Moose asked a little pointedly. Had his attitude about Kelly changed already?

"If Mr. Thompson had wanted her to have it, he would have left it to her. As it is, I'm not about to go against a dead man's wishes."

"But he was changing his will," I said. "Maybe he was going to correct that omission."

"Not according to Paul. I suppose I could turn my share over to the charity Mr. Thompson named, but really, I have no one's word but Paul's that that was his intention. At this point, I don't know what to do."

"I'm sure you'll make the right decision," I said before Moose could supply a comment of his own.

Paul Gray came back in, and he clearly wasn't very happy about the results of his telephone call. "I just got a call from Rebecca."

"Was she asking you out to lunch?" I asked.

"That would have been preferable. As a matter of fact, she just informed me that she's agreed to represent Loretta Jenkins." Paul turned to Kelly and added, "I'm afraid that it's not going to be as easy as we thought it would be."

"I'm in no hurry. Are you sure I still have a job?"

Paul nodded. "I'm the executor of the estate, and I'll need help here on this end. I see no reason not to continue your employment here at your present salary for the foreseeable future, but only if you're interested."

"There's nowhere else I'd rather be," she said.

Paul turned back to us and said, "If you don't mind, we've got a great deal of work to do here, and I don't have much time. Unfortunately, I have a full caseload back in Charlotte, so I'm going to have to squeeze every minute of my time here if this is going to work."

"We understand," I said, though Moose didn't look all that pleased about being ushered out of the office.

Once we were outside, I said, "You were pretty tough on Kelly in there. What happened to change your mind about her?"

"I finally realized that I was letting my emotions rule my behavior. You're right, Victoria. Kelly went from an innocent bystander to a prime witness in my eyes when I found out how much she was inheriting from Roy's estate."

"Then you don't buy her claim that she didn't know about the will beforehand?"

He shook his head. "Roy depended on her; that much is clear. How hard would it be for her to find out what he'd done in his will?"

"I'm still not convinced," I said.

"Hang on a second. You were the one who kept insisting that she was a suspect."

"I still think she might have done it," I admitted, "but I have no problem believing that it's possible that Roy kept this from her. I think our other suspects should still be in the running as well. After all, Asher and Sylvia had every reason to believe that he would inherit the bulk of the estate, and Mayor Mullins and James Manchester had their own reasons to want to see the man dead, too."

"Okay, I can see that. This case is driving me crazy."

"Me, too. Let's go back to the diner. At least the world makes sense there."

"I wonder about that, but it's better than hanging around here."

We never made it to the diner, though.

A police car pulled us over before we could get there.

As I saw the flashing lights, I asked my grandfather, "What did you just do?"

"Nothing," he said in protest. "I was driving the speed limit, and everything about this truck is up to code."

"Well, clearly you did something," I said as he pulled off into a parking spot.

The police car followed us in, and as I saw the officer get out, I said, "Great. Sheriff Croft is about to add a little insult to injury."

As the sheriff approached the truck, Moose hung his head out the window. "I didn't do anything wrong, and I'll fight it in court to prove it."

The sheriff smiled. "Take it easy, Moose. I just needed to get your attention. We need to have a little chat."

Moose was still aggravated; I could see it in his posture. Before he could say something we'd all regret, I said softly, "Take it easy. This could be good for us if we don't blow it."

He eased up a little, and by the time the sheriff was at the truck window, my grandfather had managed to calm himself down. "What's up?"

"Why don't we chat at the diner? I could use some coffee."

"That sounds great. We'll see you there," I said.

"Why didn't he just wait until we got there ourselves?" Moose asked me as he pulled away. "Did he have to pull me over like that on Main Street?"

"He didn't have to, but then again, he had no idea we were heading back to The Charming Moose," I said. "What's going on? Do you have any idea?"

"Not a clue," Moose said. "I guess we're going to find out pretty soon, though."

We parked at the diner, and the police cruiser did as well. I was happy to see that it was a decent distance away. As we all walked in together, Martha started to say something, but Moose just waved to her, and she stayed away. We captured a booth, and Ellen came over after I nodded in her direction.

"What can I get you?" she asked.

"Three coffees," I said.

"Is that it?"

"For now," I said. After the cups were turned over and filled, Ellen stepped back to wait on her other customers, but I noticed that she never got very far away from us.

"What's going on, Sheriff?" I asked.

"You tell me. I saw you leaving Roy Thompson's office, and I was wondering if you wouldn't mind sharing what happened there."

I put a hand lightly on Moose's arm, and he got the hint that I wanted to tell this myself. "We'd be delighted. After we bring you up to date, would you mind sharing a little with us as well? We're not asking for anything confidential. Right, Moose?"

"Right," was all that my grandfather said, and I was proud of him for letting me take the lead.

"Sounds good," the sheriff said as he took a sip of his coffee.

"Okay, here goes. Roy Thompson was about to change his will to give everything he had to charity, cutting out everyone in his life. He never had the chance to follow through, though. Someone killed him before he could make any changes."

The sheriff looked surprised to learn what we'd found out so quickly, but he didn't comment; he just nodded as he took another sip of coffee. " What exactly did the original will say?" he asked after a moment's thought.

"It splits everything down the middle, fifty-fifty, between Asher and Kelly Raven."

Sheriff Croft nearly spit his coffee out when I said the secretary's name. "You're kidding me."

"No, we heard it from the attorney handling the will himself. There's a twist, though."

"What's that?"

"Loretta Jenkins is contesting the will. Rebecca's acting as her attorney, so this isn't going to be resolved anytime soon."

"Maybe that's for the best," the sheriff said as he took another sip. Was that a grin hiding behind his mug?

"You don't look all that unhappy about the situation," I said. "Or is that just my imagination?"

"Well, we could all use more time, am I right?" he replied.

"We've only been able to eliminate two suspects so far, the only ex-convict in the bunch and our barber."

"So, you know about Chris. I was wondering if you'd figure that out. You did good work there," Sheriff Croft said. "I'm grateful for the information."

"Like Victoria said earlier, we could use a little more of that ourselves. Can you help us out?"

The sheriff considered that, and then he finally said in a soft voice, "This is not for public consumption yet, so I'd appreciate it if you'd keep it to yourselves, but maybe I can help you a little there. I can at least eliminate one of your suspects for you."

"Which one?" Moose asked eagerly. I knew that he was just as frustrated as I was about our lack of progress lately.

"We know for a fact that Barry Wilkins didn't kill him," the sheriff said, looking pleased with himself.

I'm afraid that our reaction wasn't very satisfying to him, since I had no idea who he was talking about. "Barry who?" I asked.

"You didn't know about him?" the sheriff asked, clearly perplexed by our reactions, or lack thereof.

"Barry Wilkins. He and Roy Thompson had a pretty bad blow-out in Laurel Landing the day before the murder. Barry threatened openly to kill him."

"Did he lose money, too?" Moose asked.

"On the contrary. He wanted to get in on a deal of Roy's, and the man flatly refused him. When it took off and made a small fortune for everyone who invested in it, Barry came looking for Thompson to get revenge on losing out on so much money."

"We never heard a whisper about him," I admitted. It

wasn't hard to understand, since the police had a great many more resources than we did, but it still stung a little.

"Well, it doesn't matter. He didn't do it. He was in Georgia when Roy was poisoned. Sorry about that."

"Hey, you're the pro," I said. "We're just amateurs."

"Don't sell what you do short," the sheriff said. "I'd be hard-pressed without both of you on my side every now and then."

Moose was about to say something, and I was bracing myself for what might come out of his mouth when the sheriff's radio squawked. "Sheriff, there's been an accident on old Highway 70 near the fairgrounds. The driver's hurt pretty bad. From the look of it, someone ran her off the road on purpose."

The sheriff stood quickly, and he waved in our direction as he headed for the door. Fortunately, we could still hear both sides of the conversation.

"Any ID on the victim?" he asked.

"Yeah, we just got it from the license tag. It's a woman named Loretta Jenkins."

Chapter 15

"How bad is she?" the sheriff asked as he turned around and walked back over in our direction.

"It's touch and go right now. The firefighters on the scene just about have her pried out now, and the paramedics are standing by."

"I'll be right there," he said, and then lowered the volume on his radio. "Did you hear all of that?"

"We did," I said. "I can't believe someone tried to kill Loretta. She was just in here this morning."

"Things happen," the sheriff said. "This may or may not be related to what's happening with Roy Thompson's murder."

"Sheriff, you can't believe that, can you?" I asked.

"I try not to jump to conclusions in my line of work. Anyway, I've got to run. I'll let you know how bad things are after I get there and assess the situation myself."

"Forget that," Moose said. "We're going with you."

"There's nothing that either one of you can do at the scene but get in the way," Sheriff Croft said. "Let the experts handle this."

"He's right, Moose," I said, and then I turned to the sheriff. "You promise that you'll let us know?"

"I will, but it might be a while."

"That's fine."

After he was gone, Moose said, "You gave up awfully easily just then."

"We can do more good here than at the wreck site," I said as I pulled my phone out.

"Who are you calling?" Moose asked me.

"I thought it might not be a bad idea to see if any of our suspects are away from their telephones. I know most folks use cell phones these days, but we can try landlines. The businessmen both have them, and so does Kelly. Sylvia is old fashioned enough to have one, too. What do you think?"

"I think you're brilliant," he said. "You call the women, and I'll call the men."

"What should we say if we reach any of them?" I asked.

"Just tell them what happened to Loretta. That's enough of a reason to call all of them, don't you think?"

"It sounds good to me."

I called Roy Thompson's office first, and to my surprise, Paul Gray answered the telephone himself.

"Hey, Paul. It's Victoria. May I speak with Kelly?"

In a gruff voice, he said, "She left here twenty minutes ago to run some errands for the office, but she should be back soon."

"Have her call me the second that she gets back," I said, and then I gave him the number at the diner.

"Is it urgent?" he asked.

"Not really, but I'd appreciate a return call as soon as possible. I have news. Come to think of it, it might affect you, too."

"Let's hear it, then."

"I'll tell you, but don't tell Kelly. I need to do that myself, okay?"

"That should be fine," he said after a moment's hesitation.

"Somebody just tried to kill Loretta Jenkins," I said. "They intentionally ran her car off the road, and she's in pretty rough shape right now."

"Not another one," the attorney said. "What is it with this town? Are you *all* bloodthirsty?"

"No, but we have a few bad ones around. I'm sure you have one or two in Charlotte, as well. If you didn't, there wouldn't be much business for you and your kind, now would there?"

He laughed softly. "You make a good point. Just how bad is she?"

"They're cutting her out of her car right now," I said.

"Do they have any idea about who might have done it?"

"All I know is that everything's up in the air right now."

"Well, keep in touch," he said, and then the attorney hung up on me.

I thought about where the wreck had happened, and realized that it was less than a ten minute drive from Jasper Fork. Kelly certainly had time to force Loretta off the road and head back to the office. Then again, she might just be out buying office supplies. The telephone call didn't eliminate her from our suspect list; that was all that I knew at that point.

I wasn't sure if Sylvia and her son, Asher, counted on my list or my grandfather's, but I decided to call her anyway.

The butler picked up. "Jones residence."

"May I speak with Sylvia, please?" I asked.

"I'm afraid that she's unavailable," he said.

"Okay, let's play this a different way. Is she unavailable to me, or is she just gone from the house right now?"

There was a moment's pause, and then he responded, "I suppose it wouldn't hurt to tell you that, either way, she can't speak with you at the moment."

"Listen, I'm not trying to put your job in jeopardy, but this is important. I really need to talk to her." I had a sudden thought. "Is there any way I could have her cell phone number? She would never know where I got it; I promise."

"Madam doesn't believe in them," the butler said. After another pause, he reluctantly asked, "Should I have her telephone you when she returns?"

So, he'd decided to help after all. "Yes, please." After I gave him the number, I hung up, and then I walked over to where Moose was still talking on the phone. He'd stepped aside so we wouldn't be talking over each other, but now I wanted to know what he'd found out.

He was still chatting as I sat down across from him, and from his end of the conversation, I could tell that he was talking to James Manchester. "Yes, Sir. That's fine, Sir. Thank you."

He hung up, and then Moose smiled at me. "That was quite brilliant, Victoria. I managed to catch the man in his office, and since the scene of the accident is a good forty minutes from his place of business, he's in the clear."

"How about the mayor?"

Moose grinned. "We're two for two there. Helen patched me right through when I told her that it was an emergency, and the man spent five minutes telling me exactly why he was finished taking my telephone calls now and forever. He didn't have time to run Loretta off the road and get back to his office, either. Did you have any luck on your end?"

"I couldn't confirm or deny the whereabouts of Sylvia, Asher, or Kelly," I said.

"So, then there were three," Moose said.

"Only if the person who killed Roy Thompson also ran Loretta Jenkins off the road," I answered.

"Come on, it's too big a coincidence otherwise, no matter what the sheriff said before. We have three viable suspects left on our list. How are we going to narrow the names down even further?"

"I'd like to speak with Sylvia and Asher again in person," I said.

"You're not giving up on Kelly, are you?"

"No. On our way to Sylvia's place, we're going to swing by Roy Thompson's office and check out her car."

"That's another good idea. One question, though. If Asher and Sylvia aren't back yet, why are we going to their place?"

"If we have any luck at all, they'll be back home by the time we get there."

"And if they aren't?" Moose asked.

"Then maybe we'll snoop around a little on our own."

"That's the kind of thinking I like," Moose said. "Let's go."

The problem with great ideas is that sometimes they

don't pan out. Not only was Kelly not back at the office yet, with Paul Gray's car no less, but Sylvia and Asher were still gone as well. The butler gave us that much but no more, so our snooping was cut to zero.

"What now?" Moose asked.

"I suppose the only thing we can do is to head back to Jasper Fork. We can swing past Roy's office again on our way, but otherwise, there's nothing else we can do."

"Maybe there's *one* thing," Moose said. "If someone was in a car accident, where would they go?"

"To the hospital," I said instantly.

"What if *they* weren't hurt, but what they were driving *was*?" Moose asked me with a grin.

"Then they'd probably go straight to a mechanic," I said. "Since Wayne took over Bob's shop, we should get a little more cooperation than we used to under the old ownership." I had shivers thinking about going back to the repair shop, but we didn't really have any choice.

Wayne was out front, smiling and talking to a customer, when we drove up. "Good to see you both," Wayne said after he finished speaking to his earlier visitor. "There's nothing wrong with this old beauty, is there?"

Wayne loved trucks, the older the better, and he and my grandfather had a simpatico relationship when it came to forms of transportation. "No, she's fine. We were wondering if anyone's brought in anything with body damage to it today."

Wayne nodded. "We've gotten two in, as a matter of fact," he said.

"Any chance you might tell us who owns them?" Moose asked him.

"I don't sign any confidentiality agreements with my customers, if that's what you're asking," Wayne said. He pointed to one of the bays and said, "The Jag just came in. Evidently somebody sideswiped a parked car with it."

"May we see it?" Moose asked.

"I don't see why not," Wayne replied. "How's Ellen

doing?" he asked me softly.

"She's great. You should come by the diner and see for yourself."

"Maybe I will sometime," he said with a slight grin.

Wayne walked into the bay, and my grandfather and I followed him. No one was attending to it at the moment. The door looked fairly smashed in, with extensive damage.

"Where did this happen?" Moose asked.

"They didn't tell me, but it's pretty clear that somebody got careless while they were driving. It's too nice a vehicle for that kind of treatment, if you ask me."

"Does it happen to belong to Sylvia or Asher?" I asked.

Wayne looked startled by the question. "It's one of Sylvia's. How did you know that?"

"Call it a lucky guess," I said. "What about the other one?"

"You mean the car the Jag hit? I don't know anything about that."

"No," Moose explained. "What other body job did you get in today?"

Wayne frowned, and then he said, "I don't know the fellow who owns that one. He's from out of town. Charlotte, I think."

Bingo. "By any chance, his name isn't Paul Gray, is it?"

Wayne's eyes grew wide. "Okay, now you're just freaking me out. There's no way that you could know that."

Moose said, "She's scary good. Did a young woman happen to bring it by?"

He described Kelly, and Wayne nodded. "That's the rush job. We've got to replace the whole fender, but we get a bonus if it's finished by four today. She said that she hit a tree, and I don't doubt that she scraped one pretty good. How do you both suddenly know so much about my business?"

"We're just talented, I guess," I said. "Thanks, Wayne." I had another thought, and I added, "You might want to stop doing any more work on either vehicle until the sheriff can take a look at them both."

"Why's that?" he asked, startled by my suggestion.

"Someone ran a woman named Loretta Jenkins off the road earlier today, and I have a hunch that Sheriff Croft will appreciate it if you don't destroy anything that might be evidence."

"I'll call him right now," Wayne said. "I don't need any trouble with the law."

"This should earn you some goodwill with him," I said.

"I'll take all of that I can get," he said.

I turned to Moose and said, "We need to go have a talk with Kelly right now."

We found her in Roy's office, but Paul Gray wasn't around.

"How exactly did you wreck Paul's car?" Moose asked bluntly.

She started crying the instant my grandfather said it. "I borrowed it to run errands for the company, and I wasn't used to driving it. I sideswiped a tree over near the dry cleaner. Don't tell him. I'm begging you. It will be as good as new before he knows anything about it."

"Where exactly was the tree you hit?" I asked.

"What? It was on Elm Street. Why do you want to know?"

"We need to see if there's any sign on that tree that you're telling the truth," Moose said.

She looked hurt by his accusatory words, but I noticed that her tears dried up almost instantly. "Why won't you believe me? I don't have any reason to lie."

"Because someone used a car to try to kill Loretta Jenkins," I said.

She looked shocked to hear the news. "It wasn't me! I hit a tree! You've got to believe me."

"We don't have to believe anything," Moose said. "I don't doubt that you scraped a tree, but what else did you hit? You should tell Mr. Gray what happened."

The attorney himself walked in as Moose said the last bit. "Tell me what?"

When Kelly didn't say a word, I gave her a bit of a nudge. "Either you tell him, Kelly, or my grandfather and I will."

Kelly took a deep breath, let some of it out, and then she said, "I had an accident with your car. I'm so sorry. Don't worry, it's being taken care of right now. They'll have it fixed before the day is over. Please don't be mad." She was giving it everything she had; I had to give her credit for that.

"Well, I'm afraid that it's too late for that," Paul said coldly.

"I'm getting it fixed. What's the problem?" Kelly asked a little petulantly.

"I don't give two figs about the car. You lied to me, though. I care more about someone's word than I do anything else about them."

"I *never* lied to you," Kelly said.

"Omission is a lie just as much as outright fabrication." The attorney shoved a few papers into his briefcase, and then latched it shut.

Turning to us, Paul Gray asked, "Would you be kind enough to give me a ride to the garage where my car is currently?"

"We'd be delighted," Moose said.

"But what about Roy's estate?" Kelly asked.

"I'll have an associate here tomorrow. In the meantime, I'd appreciate it if you'd turn over your keys and leave the premises immediately."

"What about my job?" she asked, the anguish clear in her voice.

"As of right now, I'm afraid that your services are no longer required here. You will receive a severance check in the mail in good time, but you're finished here."

Kelly looked shocked by how quickly things had deteriorated for her. "Is there anything that I can do to change your mind?" There was clearly more to that offer than I wanted to think about.

The attorney just shook his head. "I'm afraid not. Your keys, please."

Kelly reached into her purse and pulled out a set of keys, presumably for the office. "You can't do this to me," she said even as she handed them over to him.

"Young lady, I'm the executor of this estate. Not only am I allowed to do it, it's one of my obligations. Good day."

Kelly left, looking shell-shocked.

Even Moose was surprised. "I can't abide a liar any more than the next man, but that was harsh, even by my standards."

Paul frowned. "I didn't want to do it, but what choice did I have? I have to be able to trust whoever works on this, and she proved that I couldn't put my faith in her. It's been my experience that little lies often hide larger ones, and it's a habit that I won't tolerate. My word is my bond, and I expect others to act the same way."

"If we tell you something, you can count on it as gold," I said.

He smiled slightly. "Rebecca's already told me as much. Do you know a good locksmith? I'm afraid that I need rush service."

"Malcolm Mason is the best," I said. "Would you like me to call him for you?"

"That would be greatly appreciated," he said.

I got Malcolm on the phone. "Hey, this is Victoria. Are you busy right now?"

"I'm always overworked. What's up?"

"I need a rush job. How fast can you get to Roy Thompson's office and change the locks?"

Malcolm hesitated, and then he said, "I don't know, two, maybe three days, I guess."

That wasn't going to do at all. "I'm sorry; I didn't hear what you said."

"I'm really busy, Victoria."

"Come on, Malcolm."

"Okay," he said grudgingly. "If I move a few things around, I can be over there in half an hour."

"Ten minutes would be better," I said.

"You're killing me. You know that, don't you?"

"See you soon," I said, and then I hung up.

Paul looked a little alarmed. "I never expected you to go to such lengths on my account."

"I just wanted you to know that you can believe most of us in Jasper Fork," I said with a smile.

Moose added, "Besides, Malcolm was at the diner earlier complaining about business being so slow. He's great at what he does, but the man's got a lazy streak a mile long."

The locksmith beat my ten-minute goal by three minutes. "I happened to have them in stock, but they're going to cost you."

"I'm willing to pay any reasonable expense," Paul said. They haggled over a sum until they agreed on a price, and Malcolm got to work. He made quick work of it, and soon enough, he was on his way.

"That was relatively painless," Paul said. "Would you mind taking me to my car now?"

"Happy to do it," Moose said. "Do you mind if we make a stop along the way? I want to check out the tree at the dry cleaners she supposedly hit."

"I wouldn't mind seeing that myself," Paul said.

We parked the truck once we found the tree in question, and we all got out to examine the scraped bark.

Paul ran a hand over it. "It doesn't look too bad."

"Honestly, I don't know how to judge it," Moose said. "The way they make cars these days, it doesn't take all that much to total them."

The attorney looked a little unsettled by that statement, and he was on edge until we got to the shop.

Wayne was surprised to see us so soon. "Back already?"

"Here's the owner of the other car you got in today," Moose said. "He wants a look at the damage."

Wayne shook the attorney's hand. "You need a new

front left fender, but there was one at the parts warehouse, so I can have you fixed up in no time. Like I told your assistant earlier, it's cheaper to pop a new one on this model than it is to try to repair the old one. She was going to pay cash. Is that still the way you'd like to handle it?"

He shook his head. "Call this number. My insurance company will take care of you."

Wayne shrugged as he pocketed the card. "That's fine. It's all the same to me."

"When will it be finished?" Paul asked.

"If it weren't for the sheriff, I'd be done with it by the end of the day," Wayne told him.

Paul looked surprised to hear that, and I suddenly realized that we hadn't told him about the possibility that Kelly had used his car in an attempted vehicular homicide.

After I brought him up to speed, Paul frowned, and then he asked Wayne, "Do you have a vehicle I can rent in the meantime?"

"We'll be glad to take you wherever you need to go," Moose said.

"I appreciate the offer, but I'm going back to my office in Charlotte. My associate will make the trade-off when he comes to take over here for me."

"Rebecca will be disappointed to hear that you're leaving," I said.

Paul shook his head. "No more than I am. I won't give up on her that easily, though," he added with a grin.

"That sounds good. I'm betting that she'll appreciate your efforts."

We left Paul Gray at the garage and headed back to the diner. Moose and I still wanted to speak with Sylvia and Asher, but if they kept dodging us, we didn't have much choice but to bide our time.

As for Kelly, she was now a prime suspect, more than ever, in fact.

Chapter 16

"There you are," Sylvia Jones said breathlessly as we got out of the truck back at the diner. "I've been waiting for you forever!"

"What a coincidence," Moose said. "We've been looking for you, too. We hear you were in an accident today."

"What? Who told you that? I'm fine."

"You're car is in the shop right now," I said.

Sylvia waved a hand at us dismissively. "Asher must have done it. Why am I not surprised that he didn't tell me about it? Moose, Victoria, you've got to do something about him. I hate to say it, but my son has lost his mind. He's dangerous!"

"Calm down, Sylvia," Moose said. "Would you like to come in and tell us what happened?"

"I can't," she said as she looked wildly around the parking lot. "It's not safe."

"It will be safer inside than it is standing out here in the open," I said. "If Asher comes into the diner, we'll protect you."

"Do you promise?" she asked. "I hate not feeling protected from my own son."

"We'll look out for you," Moose said.

When we walked in, Moose nodded toward Martha, but we didn't stop to chat. My grandmother read the clue beautifully again and gave us our space. Moose led us back to a booth near the kitchen, and I approved of his choice. We could all sneak back there in a heartbeat if Asher approached, and I didn't care how crazy he might be; I doubted that he'd tackle Greg when my husband had access to so many sharp and dangerous weapons.

I fetched us all coffee, and after Sylvia took a big gulp of hers, Moose said, "Tell us what happened."

"When Asher found out about Loretta last night, he snapped. He told me that he was going to scare her off if it was the last thing he did, but when he came back to the house later, he said that it had backfired. Evidently Loretta is more like her father than any of us originally thought."

"So, you believe her story?" I asked.

"What, that Roy was her father? There's no doubt in my mind that it's entirely possible. After all, my ex-husband wasn't known for his self restraint."

"What exactly did Asher say today that has upset you so much?" Moose asked.

"He was ranting like a lunatic about her all morning, and nothing I could say helped. I urged him to let the attorneys handle it, but he took it as a personal affront that she was going to share in his inheritance. Asher kept asking me why he should share it all with anyone else, since he'd been the one who'd done all of the work."

What an odd thing to say. "Did you have any idea what he meant by that?"

"He couldn't have killed his own father," Sylvia said without the slightest conviction in her voice. "It's impossible."

I wasn't so sure, but this wasn't the time or place to bring that up. There were more pressing things to deal with at the moment. "He couldn't have been all that happy about Kelly Raven inheriting half of it all, either," I said.

Sylvia shook her head. "If I were her, I'd hire a bodyguard, or maybe even two. Asher said that after he's done with his sister, he's going after her. He isn't planning on sharing Roy's estate with anyone."

"But legally, there's nothing he can do about that," Moose said.

Sylvia looked as though she were about to cry. "I told him that, and he said that if the judicial system wouldn't see things his way, he'd take care of everything himself. After he said that, Asher grabbed the keys to my Jaguar and stormed out. I thought he'd gone out to blow off some steam, but then I heard about what happened to Loretta on the radio." Sylvia drank a little more coffee, and then she asked, "Is it bad?"

"She might die," I said. It was a fair assessment, based on what we'd heard over the sheriff's radio.

"Oh, no. What am I going to do?"

"We need to call the sheriff," Moose said. "And I mean right now."

"He's probably still at the accident scene," I said.

"I have a hunch that he'll come running if he hears what Sylvia has to say about her son. Go ahead and call him, Victoria."

I nodded, but before I dialed, I asked Sylvia, "Are you sure that you're okay with this?"

"I can't handle him anymore myself," she said, and she finally started to quietly cry next to me.

Sheriff Croft picked up on the second ring and said, "Victoria, I was just about to come by the diner. I'm not a minute away. Can it wait until I get there?"

"That's fine. We'll tell you then."

"Tell me what?" he asked.

"It's about Asher."

"Hang on. I'll be there in a second."

The sheriff took nearly a minute to make it to The Charming Moose, and the second he walked in, he spotted us and walked straight to our booth in back. "What's going on?"

"Do you want to tell him, or should we?" I asked Sylvia.

"It's my son," she said as she dabbed at her tears. "He's lost his mind. I'm afraid of what he might have done, or what he might still do."

"Explain," the sheriff said.

Sylvia did a credible job of bringing him up to speed, with just a few interjections from my grandfather and me. She finally ended with, "You've got to find him and stop him."

"We'll do our best," Sheriff Croft said. He stood and

moved away from us so he could have some privacy.

"Will he be able to find Asher, do you think?" Sylvia asked.

"He's very good at what he does," I replied, trying my best to reassure her. I was glad she hadn't added anything to her question. I'd been thinking the same thing myself, only my question had been, 'Will he be able to find him in time?' I wasn't one of Kelly's biggest fans, but I was now fearful for her life. I took a chance and called her number, but there was no answer. If she had Caller-ID—and who didn't these days—it wouldn't surprise me at all if she'd declined to pick up when she saw who was calling her. I left a quick message telling her to find the sheriff, no matter what, and hoped that I'd been able to reach her time. Moose had listened in as I'd left the message, and he nodded his approval as I hung up. "That's good thinking."

"Asher wouldn't really hurt her," Sylvia said aloud, no doubt more to convince herself than the two of us.

"We're just taking every precaution," Moose said. There was a reassuring tone to his voice that always amazed me. How did he do that?

The sheriff walked back over to us, and I told him, "I just called Kelly Raven, but she didn't pick up."

"I've got a man on his way to her apartment right now," Sheriff Croft said.

"What about my boy?" Sylvia asked.

"I've got officers out looking for him, too. That's all we can do right now."

"How's Loretta doing?" Moose asked.

"It's still touch and go," the sheriff said. "There's no doubt that it was deliberate, though. Somebody wanted her dead."

"How do you know that?" I asked.

"There were no skid marks at the crime scene except hers, and from the look of her car, I've got a feeling that she was tapped more than once before her car finally went over that embankment."

It just amazed me what people could do when they were driven by greed. How much was another life worth? How about two or three?

"If that's it, I'm going out on patrol myself," the sheriff said. "First, I have to stop by the garage and have a look at those cars, though." His radio squawked, and he said, "Excuse me," as he stepped aside.

"What's that all about?" Sylvia asked hopefully. "Have they found my Asher?"

"We'll know in a second," I said.

The sheriff walked back, and from the troubled frown on his face, it was clear that the news hadn't been good.

"What is it?" I asked.

"Kelly Raven's apartment door was standing wide open when my officer got to the scene. It appears that there was some kind of struggle there."

"Was it Asher?" Sylvia asked, the dread thick in her voice.

"We have no idea. There were no witnesses. I've *really* got to go now."

"What about me?" Sylvia shrieked. "You can't just leave me here alone! He might come after me next."

The sheriff shrugged. "I can't do anything except lock you up in one of my cells for your own protection. I don't have a single officer I can spare to look after you right now."

"You want me to go to jail? I won't!" she said adamantly.

"Are there any friends you could call?" he asked. It was clear that there were other things the sheriff would rather be doing than babysitting Sylvia Jones.

"To harbor me and keep me safe? No, there's no one."

How sad was that? I was about to offer her our sanctuary at the diner when Moose said, "Come on, Sylvia, I know that you're friends with Anita Bidwell. Call her."

"I couldn't," Sylvia said. "How can I explain what's happening?"

"You'll find the words. I've got a better idea. Why don't

I just take you over there in my truck? She'll have a harder time turning you down if you just show up on her doorstep."

"Are you suggesting that I visit her without even phoning first?" Sylvia looked even more horrified by that prospect than she'd been about spending time locked up in jail.

"You don't have much choice, Sylvia," I said.

"It's as good a plan as any," the sheriff said.

"I don't suppose I have any real choice, do I?" she asked.

"It's going to be all right," he told her, and then my grandfather turned to me and added, "I'll be back before long."

"Be careful," I answered.

Two minutes after they left, my cell phone rang.

It was Wayne at the garage. "Hey, Victoria. Do you have a minute?"

"Sure, always for you," I said.

"Would you mind coming over to the shop? There's something here you should see."

"Can you give me a hint what it is?" I asked. I didn't like going anywhere without Moose when it concerned the case we were investigating.

"Believe me; you're going to want to see this for yourself. It's easier to just show you than to explain it to you, if you know what I mean."

I made an executive decision right then and there. After all, the repair shop was out in the open. How dangerous could it be going by myself? "I'll be there in five minutes," I said.

"That's great," he answered.

As I approached the front, Martha asked, "Victoria, are you leaving so soon?"

"I'm going to go see Wayne at the repair shop," I said. "Send Moose over there when he gets back, would you?"

"I'd be happy to. Should I have him call you first?"

I pulled out my telephone and saw that it was nearly out of its charge. "Do me a favor and put that in the charger for me, would you? I'll pick it up when I get back."

"Do you want mine in the meantime?" she asked.

"Since when did you start carrying a cell phone around with you?"

"Don't tell your grandfather," she said with a grin. "I'm going to keep it a secret as long as I can."

"He won't hear it from me. Thanks, but I'm sure that I'll be fine," I said.

"I hate to sound ungrateful, Wayne, but have you told the sheriff what you're about to share with me?"

The mechanic grinned as he wiped his hands on a rag. "He's the one who suggested that I call you. He's well aware of what I found."

"Then I'd love to see it."

"Follow me," Wayne said.

We walked into the service area, and I noticed that two cars were on lifts, side by side at the same level. One was pointed in one direction, while the other one was just the opposite.

"What am I supposed to be looking at?" I asked as I studied both cars.

"One belongs to the Jones family, and the other one is Paul Gray's vehicle. Look a little closer. Don't you see it?" Wayne asked.

"All I see are two cars. One has a dented front fender, and the other has a busted back one."

Wayne nodded. "That's all true enough, but try to imagine how they might have happened. Study both fenders, and take your time."

I looked, but I really didn't see anything. "I'm not sure why I'm doing this. One hit a tree and a car, and the other sideswiped a parked car. What do they have in common?"

Wayne stepped between the cars as he explained, "This is the front left fender, and this is the right rear."

"Okay, I can see that much."

"Now look closer."

I stepped up, and studied one ding, and then the other.

"The paint on this fender matches the paint on that one," I said.

"Excellent," Wayne said as he nodded in approval.

"So, does that mean that Kelly hit Asher while she was driving Paul Gray's car?"

"Not necessarily. Asher could have just as easily have hit the car Kelly was driving. There's no way to tell, based on the impact."

"Why would one of my suspects hit the other one?" I thought about the possibilities, and then I said, "Hang on a second. If these cars hit each other, who knocked Loretta Jenkins off the road?"

"We won't know that until the police lab does a lot more tests. The sheriff's going to confiscate both fenders for further analysis, but at this point, there's no visual evidence that either one of them hit the Jenkins car."

"Is there any chance that the car that hit Loretta's tried to scrape the paint off onto the other car?"

Wayne laughed. "What are you, a cop? That's exactly what the sheriff asked."

I felt pleased to hear the compliment. "And what did you tell him?"

"Some paint might have transferred, but they shouldn't have any problem determining which vehicle hit the Jenkins car."

"How long will that take?" I asked.

"I have no idea. All I know is that as soon as I get each fender removed, I'm supposed to call the sheriff back so he can pick them up and send them to Raleigh for analysis."

"So, it won't be anytime soon, then," I said.

"Hey, I'm just a simple mechanic," Wayne said as he spread his hands out. "I have no idea."

"I kind of doubt that," I said. "What's your hunch? Do you have one?"

"I have a guess, but I'm not one hundred percent sure, so I hate to say it out loud. Do you know what I mean? I might be damaging someone's reputation here."

"Don't worry. Right now I believe that either one of them could have done it, so you won't be sullying anything in my eyes."

"I understand that, but I'd still rather not say."

"I can respect that," I said. "Thanks for the show."

"You're welcome. For what it's worth, I hope you catch the bad guy."

"That makes two of us," I said. Things still didn't make sense, and I knew that I was running out of time.

Chapter 17

Instead of going straight back to the diner, I decided to take a drive and try to come up with a solution that explained the whirlwind of facts swarming around my mind. After wandering aimlessly around for twenty minutes, I figured that it would make more sense for me to just head home. After all, my backyard was my perfect oasis away from the world, and I could really think there. I might even light a fire on the new propane fire pit. Dancing flames had a way of stimulating my thoughts sometimes. And in the end, what could it hurt? At least I'd get to have a fire. When I got there, though, I couldn't find the long matches Greg had bought especially for lighting the fire, and I didn't feel like going inside to hunt around for them. I played with one of the green propane cylinders, tossing it from hand to hand as I pondered all of the possibilities. It was warm enough sitting in the sun, anyway. We'd need a fire tonight if we came out, but for now, just sitting by the pit was enough.

I had a hunch that I had all of the facts I needed to figure this mess out, if I were only clever enough to come up with the killer. The key had to be somewhere in the accident that had forced Loretta Jenkins off that road this morning. It was clear, at least to me, that it had to be one of our final suspects, Kelly or Asher. I was leaning toward Asher at the moment, but I had to wonder if he could actually kill his own father. I knew that it was a popular theme in mythology, but in real life, I just couldn't buy it. Could someone else have done it for him, though? What about Sylvia? She'd certainly seemed afraid earlier when she'd come by the diner, but her fear of her son could be real enough to explain her behavior. What if Asher had discovered that his mother had killed Roy Thompson for him? It might just be enough to drive him over the edge. Then Asher could have gone after Loretta, not so much for the money, but for trying to steal what he regarded as his birthright. If that were the case, though, why hadn't he made an attempt on Kelly's life yet? After all, she was getting half of the estate if the current will made it through probate. Did that explain the struggle at her apartment? Or was there another, more sinister, reason that he'd saved Kelly for last? Then I remembered that I'd seen Asher near the diner when Kelly had visited us there earlier. Had he been waiting to talk to my grandfather and me, or Kelly? When she left, she'd said that she had an appointment she'd forgotten about. Could it have been with Asher, her partner in crime?

Why not? Things suddenly started to fall into place. Asher and Kelly both had a great deal to gain by Roy Thompson's death if they knew about his last will and testament, and the fact that it was about to be changed would be something they would each want to stop. The two of them would have both lost fortunes, and I knew that stranger conspiracies had been founded on a great deal less in the past.

Suspecting it and proving it were two different things, though.

I had to wonder if my grandfather and I could trap one of them into confessing. I'd go back to the diner and get Moose, and we'd give it our best try.

I never got the chance, though.

Asher came around the side of the house as I was getting ready to head back out, and before I even had a chance to react, I had a gun pointed straight at my heart.

"What are you doing, Asher?" I asked as he gestured for me to go back toward the fire pit. I had no choice but to obey.

"Drop the act, Victoria. I saw you at the auto repair shop before, and then I followed you around until you came back here. It's pretty obvious that you know that I'm the one who forced my so-called sister off the road today."

"Actually, Kelly did a fairly good job of trying to protect you there. When she rammed your car with Paul Gray's vehicle, flecks of paint lodged on both fenders. It might not be enough to get you off in court, but then again, there's a legitimate shadow of doubt that she planted there. You got lucky when you chose your partner in crime. My guess is that she's been running the show from the start."

Kelly must have been waiting out of sight in the bushes, because when I said her name, she knew that I realized that she was a part of this murder conspiracy, so she stepped out and joined us.

At least she was unarmed. "You're smarter than I gave you credit for, Victoria," Kelly said. "How did you know that I was in on it?"

"It's the only way it all made sense. You must have stumbled upon Roy's will at some point. And why wouldn't you? After all, you had access to everything the man did. I'm guessing that when Roy told you to summon Paul Gray and bring witnesses with him, you knew that the riches you'd been holding out for were all about to disappear. Did you approach Asher with your plan, or did he think of it himself?"

"We decided together that my father had to go," Asher said indignantly. It was clear that the man was constantly being manipulated by women, first his mother, and then Kelly.

"Fine, whatever you say, Asher," I said. I always made it a point never to argue with a man holding a gun on me.

I had nothing to lose, and at least maybe I'd be able to discover the truth if I pushed them both a little now. It would be little solace, but at least I wouldn't die of curiosity. "Kelly, I'm guessing you're the one who poisoned the cake. It's hard for me to imagine that a man could kill his own father in cold blood like that."

"Whether I did it or not, good luck proving it. I'm willing to bet that no one even saw me at the festival," Kelly said.

"You had time, though, didn't you? I'm sure that no one noticed that you were gone from the office, but if we go through the photos the police collected, I'm willing to wager that you turn up somewhere, unless you were smart enough to disguise yourself."

She smiled as I said it, so I had a hunch that I was right on the money. "As I say, this is all speculation on your part. It will be impossible to establish any of that."

"Maybe so, but with Asher's testimony, I don't need to prove anything."

"We're partners," Kelly said with a hard laugh. "If I go down, he knows that I'll take him with me."

"Does that include the plan to get rid of Loretta Jenkins, too? That was a pretty desperate act, wouldn't you say? Actually, it was the only sloppy part of your entire plan."

"Asher did that all on his own; I can assure you of that."

"She had to go! There was no way I was going to let her mess up our perfect plan. Why didn't you just use your new fire pit, Victoria?" Asher asked a little petulantly as he looked at me. "It would have saved us all from this mess."

"What did you to do to our pit?" I asked, thinking about how close I'd come to lighting it half an hour earlier.

"The first match you struck would have been your last," Asher said with a little too much pride for my comfort. "Now we have to do it ourselves."

I had to move fast, and I had to do it now.

The small propane tank I'd been playing with earlier was within my reach, and I hoped that if I could throw it at Asher long enough to distract him, maybe I could make it to the woods behind our house before he could recover.

It wasn't much of a plan, but it was all that I had.

But first I had to say something that would get that gun off me. "Kelly's going to kill you after you get rid of me. You know that, don't you, Asher?"

"Don't listen to her. You know that I wouldn't do that. Like I said, we're partners," Kelly said, doing her best to reassure him of her intentions.

"Think about it. People around her seem to keep ending up dead. Did you notice that, Asher?"

"You don't understand. I would have been willing to wait, but Dad *had* to die," he said. "He was going to ruin everything when he wanted to change his will."

I had no idea if what I was about to say was true or not, but that didn't matter at this point. Every time Asher spoke to Kelly, the gun pointed toward her as well. I needed to use that to my advantage. "You could have challenged the new will yourself in court. After all, you have legal standing. Kelly would have been out in the cold, though. You didn't need to kill your father, Asher. All you had to do was just wait for him to die."

"Is that true?" Asher asked Kelly as he pointed the gun toward her subconsciously.

I couldn't afford to wait for her to respond. I knew how slick Kelly was, and if I hesitated now, the next order she'd give him would be to shoot me.

I reached down, picked up the cylinder, and threw it straight at Asher.

It didn't hit him directly, but it did manage to startle him enough to make him drop his gun on the ground. I planned to let the two of them fight for it while I was running for my life.

I never made it two steps into the woods.

"Both of you stay right where you are!" Kelly barked. I looked back to see that she was now holding a small-caliber pistol in her hand, and more significantly, she was fanning it between the two of us.

"What are you doing?" Asher asked. He was clearly outraged by the new dynamic of the situation. I wasn't sure if I was any better off now, but I wasn't any worse off, either.

"Asher, you're becoming more of a liability than an asset," Kelly said. "If I play this right, I can get rid of both of you. Here's how this is going to play out. Asher, it's going to look as though you shot Victoria, but not before she managed to get off a kill shot of her own."

I had to give Asher credit. Whether it was through rage or a strong sense of self preservation, he lashed out at her in an instant.

Without hesitation, Kelly shot him in the chest at fairly close range.

I couldn't stay to see how he was.

Asher was on his own now; I had to try to save myself.

The caliber of Kelly's gun looked small enough so that I figured if I could put some distance between us, I might still get out of this alive.

I started for the woods when I heard a familiar voice call out behind us all, "Drop the weapon, Kelly. You have two seconds, and then I'm putting you down."

There was no doubt, no hesitation in the sheriff's voice, and after a moment, I turned to see Kelly do exactly as she was told.

"How did you find me?" I asked the sheriff as he handcuffed Kelly. Asher wasn't going anywhere, at least not at the moment, but the sheriff did kick both guns well away from the man's reach before he turned to take care of Kelly.

The sheriff explained, "Moose got back from delivering Sylvia to her friend's house, and Martha told him where you'd gone. Your grandfather called Wayne at the garage, and that triggered a manhunt. We had every cruiser we have out looking for you, as well as every last member of your family with a driver's license. I had confidence that one of us would find you."

"I'm just glad you did it in time," I said.

"I've got to give you credit, Victoria. You figured it all out before I did."

"I'm just sorry that I didn't do it in time to tell you before Asher got shot," I said.

"Speaking of Asher, could you watch him for me for a minute? I need to get Kelly into my squad car."

I looked at the man, lying on the grass. "Is he even still alive?"

There was a moan then, and he tried to sit up.

"You shot me!" he said to Kelly, as though he were accusing her of stealing his toy train.

"Not very accurately, apparently," Kelly said as she was led away.

I walked over and looked down at Asher. "Are you going to give me any trouble, or am I going to have to shoot you, too?"

Asher immediately laid back down where he was, and after that, he made no more attempts to move until the ambulance arrived.

I was glad for that.

I wasn't sure that I would have had the heart to kick him, let alone shoot the man.

Two hours later I was back at The Charming Moose, surrounded by my family and friends, telling the whole story again for the third time.

The sheriff walked in and joined our little private party, and as he approached, he asked, "Victoria, do you have a second?"

"Absolutely," I said. "What's up?"

"I just wanted to let you know that Asher's going to be okay. He just got out of surgery, but before he'd let them put him under, he insisted that he tell me about what he'd done to your fire pit. It's a good thing Kelly was using such a small-caliber handgun. It could have been a lot worse."

"Has he confessed to what they did?" I asked.

"They both have," the sheriff said with a grin. "It's going to be up to the district attorney which one to charge with the harshest penalty, but I have full confidence that they're both going down."

"I'm glad. To think that it all came about because of greed. What's going to happen to Roy Thompson's estate now?"

"I just spoke with someone in Charlotte named Paul Gray, and he assured me that it will all go to the named secondary beneficiary, which also happens to be the society Roy was going to change his will to when this whole mess started."

"Does Kelly know that yet?" I asked with a wicked grin.

"Actually, I was just about to go tell her, unless you'd like the honors yourself."

"Thanks, but I'll pass. Honestly, I don't want to see her again until I'm testifying against her at her trial."

"I understand that completely. Now, I'll leave you to your little party."

"Why don't you stay?" Greg asked as he approached us. "We've got a lot to celebrate."

"I appreciate the offer, but there's still a great deal of work to be done."

After the sheriff was gone, Greg hugged me tightly. "I can't believe how close I came to losing you again. You're making too much of a habit of this, Victoria."

"Hey, it's not by choice, believe me."

Moose came over and tapped my husband on the shoulder. "Don't go hogging her, Greg. Give somebody else a turn." As my grandfather embraced me, I could almost feel my ribs cracking, but I didn't mind in the least.

I was right back where I belonged, surrounded by the people I loved most in the world.

As far as I was concerned, he could crack away.

It was good to be right where I belonged, and to appreciate every moment of it.

CPSIA information can be obtained at www.ICGtesting.com
Printed in the USA
LVOW051535190213

320796LV00001B/231/P